FERN

OUTCAST

THE JOURNEY OF A LEPER'S DAUGHTER

EQUIP PRESS

Colorado Springs

Outcast, The Journey of a Leper's Daughter
Copyright © 2023 Fern Reynolds

First Edition: 2023
Outcast / Fern Reynolds
Paperback ISBN: 978-1-958585-15-3
eBook ISBN: 978-1-958585-16-0

OUTCAST

DUSTY ROADS

The long dusty road seems endless. Mam says we are going to Jaipur. She says it will take months to walk there.

The dust cakes on my bare feet. I look down at my feet and remember my sadness when Naniji kicked me out of the house. She wouldn't even give me time to get my shoes.

I am tired. I am thirsty. The grumblings of my stomach have stopped. I guess it knows there is nothing to give it, so it stopped complaining.

Mam does her best to give us food but most days she puts grass and rocks in our pot with water and that is our soup.

Oh, what I wouldn't give for my Naniji's naan and butter chicken right now, or her yummy Kheer, Indian rice pudding, or Unniyappam, fried banana and rice flour balls. I would even be happy for just a cup of hot masala tea.

We have been walking for days. It is hot. There is no

shade because we are in a desert area.

I turned thirteen two days before this all started. I was excited because as soon as I became a woman, I would have married Anrit.

But now everything has changed.

It has been a year. Tomorrow I will turn fourteen. There will be no party. There will be no wedding.

I still don't understand everything that has happened. I can't ask questions. If I do my parents will slap me.

I wonder, "How did we get here, walking on these dirt roads with no shoes?"

I long for life the way it used to be.

* * * * * * * * * * * * *

Each Day Begins Like Any Other

Before this journey started, I wake up before the sun rises. Every morning, I hear drums beating loudly.

Mam says it's because the priests are waking up the gods. She says that we must help by saying our pujas (prayers) very loudly to help wake them up.

"We want them to be fully awake when we do our morning devotionals," she explains, "so they will listen and give us a good day."

Now that I am ten, I sometimes don't hear the drums anymore. I hope the gods don't get mad at me for not waking them up.

Once I am up, Mam gives me a glass of milk. I drink it quickly. Mam has already been up and bought the grain for the skinny cow that roams the street right outside our gate. She gives me grain and I run out and place it in front of the cow, who is one of our ancestors, a god. The cow was chewing on trash that is left in the street but turns and accepts the grain. We hope this act of worship will help the cow to have a good day and that she will in turn bestow good fortune on us.

I hurry back into the house. Mam and Naniji are about to light the incense and put the small cakes in front of the statue of Ganesh and Shiva. We start our chants and offer our sacrifice of incense to them. Again, we pray they will bestow good fortune on us.

While we are chanting and rocking back and forth with our eyes closed I sometimes open my eyes to see if the gods will respond. I've never seen them eat the cakes we offer to them. How do these marble carvings bless me each day? Where are they when Sheba steals my lunch at school?

After this time of worship, we carefully wash the statues and place them back in their boxes. Mam takes kajal, a mixture of black lead and almond oil that she grinds every day and draws a black line around my baby brother's eye. It will keep the evil eye away and infections away from the baby's eyes.

She grabs Sumit, my elder brother, and my wrists to check for the bracelet we wear. Mam made these for us. My bracelet has purple beads and Sumit's has blue beads. In the middle of the string is a bead that looks like an eye. This bracelet brings us good luck and protects us from anything bad that could happen to us. It's supposed to keep people from cursing us with their evil looks.

Now it is time for morning chores and breakfast. My chore is to sweep our rooms and the veranda. I have a broom made of straw. I think it stirs up more dust than it sweeps up dirt. I have a piece of plastic that Papa found on the road. I use that to scoop up the dirt and throw it out.

Mam has breakfast ready. I have chai or masala tea. Our breakfast is usually the same as our lunch and dinner. We will have a flatbread called *roti*, thin lentil crepes called *dosas* or steamed rice-dough pancakes called *idlis*, along with different dips and chutneys. We sometimes have spiced potatoes. Mam packs our lunches, the same meal, in tin cups that stack on top of each other. The handle pulls up and holds them in place.

I have several sets of clothes and one school uniform. Most of the time I have two pair of shoes.

When I was four, I got my first pair of shoes. That was because I started school. I only wore those shoes to school. As soon as I came home, I took them off, wiped them off with a dry cloth, and put them in the place by the door where we store our shoes. We don't wear shoes inside, even in the stores. Everyone takes their shoes off at the door. The shoes have more germs on them than a toilet seat and out of respect, we avoid tracking in germs.

When I was eight, my feet had outgrown my school shoes. My parents did not have the money to buy me a pair of shoes because they had bought my brother his. I had to go to school without shoes for a couple of weeks until my teacher called my papa and told him I have to wear the uniform shoes. The next day, Mam bought me a pair two sizes too big so I would have them for at least another year.

Mam kept my hair short until I turned eight. Now, at eleven, it is down past my back. Mam mutters that every time I go to school I get lice. She puts coconut oil in my hair and pulls it tightly back in a ponytail. But some days, she is too busy and I wear my hair down. That's when I get lice.

Mam pulls the crawling bugs out of my hair as she combs the coconut oil through it. Today she seems too tired to pick out the nits. I hope she will do it tonight because my head itches.

GOING TO SCHOOL

I t is time for school," Mam announces as she puts a small bundle of food in a tin container for me.

That will be my lunch while at school with my friends.

We go to school every day except Sunday. Our school day starts at 8:00 am in the morning and is over at 4:00 pm. On Saturday we get out early at 2:00 pm.

I'm dressed in my school uniform, which is a jumper that comes to my knees. My blouse underneath is white. I have a tie that hangs down the front and covers the buttons of my shirt. We wear socks that go to our knees and black shoes. It's funny that we don't like the British or the influence they left after leaving in 1948, but we still dress like them and run our schools as they told us to.

Mam stops me as I walk to the front door. She has a wet cloth and quickly rubs my face and extra-hard behind my ears.

My girlfriends are waiting for me as I come out of my house. We hold hands and skip our way to school.

We try to avoid the naughty boys who like to tease us or throw dirt at us. But we like to watch the nice boys and we always giggle when they turn and look our way.

I like school. I like to do my work in my workbooks. But some days are hard. It is a government school, not a public school. I wish I could go to a public school like my brother. But you have to pay for that privilege. It costs 150 rupees a month. In America that would be $2.00. My family does not have that money for me since I am a girl. My parents pay for my brother to go to a public school.

Sometimes our teachers show up and sometimes they do not. Sometimes they will teach us if they are the young pretty women who are just out of university. The men never teach, they sit and drink from their square bottles. By the end of the day, my teacher can barely walk out of the school building.

So I do as much as I can from my workbook.

I like math. It makes sense to me, most of the time. Last week I came across a problem I didn't understand. I went up to the teacher's desk.

I asked, "Sir, could you explain this problem to me?"

He frowned at me. "You're a girl," he said. "Don't trouble yourself with that. You don't need to understand it."

I stood there. "But I'd like to understand it."

My teacher grabbed his switch and started hitting me.

I ran back to my seat. The other kids just laughed while I quietly cried.

When I get home, my brother will help me with my math problems. He tutors me. I am thankful that he helps me. But he does say that when I get to be thirteen he will stop since I won't need to know any more because I will be getting married and all that I will need to worry about is tending to my family.

That makes me sad. I want to do much more. Will that be possible?

DAILY LIFE IN OUR VILLAGE

Our daily life in the village centers around meals. Most Hindus are vegetarians. We are most of the time, but we will eat chicken meat when Papa brings one home from the market. I love it when we get to eat cashew curry chicken, butter chicken or chicken tikka masala. But, my favorite is *Biryani*, a spiced rice and chicken dish with eggs and potatoes.

When we cook with Naniji, first, we gather sticks for the fire. My job is to go out and find sticks. We keep a pile on the back wall. Our outdoor tandoori oven is a clay oven in the middle of the courtyard that my grandfather built. My mam puts the sticks in the hole, and if we have matches, we use them to start the fire. If not, Naniji uses flint rocks, hitting them together, to cause a spark for the fire. While she is doing this Mam goes over to the hand-cranked sewing machine and mends some of my papa's shirts. I keep stoking the fire while Mam does her mending.

Naniji puts flour that she has ground, water, yogurt and yeast in a big brass bowl. She mixes it with her hands, pouring water in slowly to get the right consistency. Then she starts kneading the dough. She will do this for ten to fifteen minutes to get it just right.

She rolls the dough into balls. Naniji smashes out each ball and slaps it back and forth to make a flat disc. Mam stops her sewing and goes to help. They have about fifteen balls to make. I will be able to help them when I can do it without dropping one on the dirt floor. After the naan cooks, they pull each one out, rub butter on it and stack them in the pan. Sometimes they add garlic. My favorite!

The fire dies down and they place each disc inside of the oven where they stick. The disc will puff up a little and fall to the bottom in the ashes. They pull the naan out with a long tong. Each one takes three to four minutes to cook. When they are finished, they wrap them in a white cloth, put them in a round plastic pot and lock the lid on the pot. *Mmmm.*

My earliest memory is playing in the courtyard with my cousin and my brother while Mam and Naniji cooked. I was five and Sumit was seven. Our cousin, who is also the eldest boy, was eight. We would play kick ball or tag. It was fun to be together.

We could smell the food Mam and Naniji were making. Sometimes they would give us a taste or a little *lassi* before dinner! Lassi is a blend of yogurt, water, spices, and sometimes fruit. The mango lassi is my favorite. But we only get it two months out of the year, during the mango growing season. I really like the banana lassi, too!

Since I turned twelve, my brother and cousins do not let me play ball with them anymore. Instead, I help Mam with sewing now.

I look forward to Saturday evenings. Now that I am twelve I get to cook a large meal for our family with Mam, Naniji and my aunties. It's the same meal we eat every day, except on Saturdays we sometimes get to have a sweet treat made with jaggery, a powder Mam grinds from the sugar cane she gathers from our field out back

After dinner Mam boils water and brings in the big tub. We all get to bathe. Papa goes first, then my brother and my baby brother. Mam is next. I am last and by the time I get in the tub, the water is cold and not so clean. I loved the baths, it felt good to dip my whole body into the water, and then Naniji would scrub my body with soap she had made. It had a lavender smell and I always loved to breathe it all in.

I have a set of play clothes: that are a *punjabi* suits, a *saree* for special occasions like going to the temple or a wedding, and a set of school clothes. I have a couple of other punjabi suits that I wear for visits or going to the market.

On Saturday my chore is to wash our clothes. I wash the clothes I wore that week and my school uniform. Next week I will wear another set of clothes. I wash my mam's *saree* she wears all week. Mam has other sarees but she just wears one all week. She sleeps in her saree too, never taking it off until Saturday for her bath. I also wash my papa's pants and *lungees*, my brother's two sets of school uniforms, and his pants and lungees. Papa and Sumit wear a new set of clothes each day. But they only wear the same lungee each week since they put it on each evening. The lungees and sarees are hard to wash because they are so long. Sometimes I get twisted up in them. Papa wraps his lungee around like a skirt, but Sumit likes to tuck his up between his legs like a big diaper . . . just like the old men in town.

I walk down to the river with my basket full of these clothes. I have some soap my mam made. And I have a bowl of ash. I take each piece and dip it in the river, then I scrub it with the ash. I rinse it and then scrub it again with the soap. Again, I rinse. I do this with each piece. I lay each piece on a big boulder to dry.

It is very hot. I take a few sips of the river water as I work.

When I am finished, I sit on a boulder and wait for the clothes to dry. Sometimes I have a little food to eat that I brought from home. Sometimes my friends are also there, and we will play a game of tag or throw rocks into the river. Many times I will see a cow lumber down to the river. She will walk in and drink the water, pee and poop, too. At times there could be several cows together. I often see the dead carcass of an animal float by. Sometimes, I see a funeral pyre floating by, still smoldering. I stop and offer a prayer to Ganesh or one of the other gods and hope that the person's soul has been reincarnated to another better place. Mam tells me that doing this will give me a better chance to be reincarnated in a higher caste in my next life.

After the clothes are almost dry, I gather them in my basket and take them back to the house. My uncle irons the clothes, as he has since he was eighteen, when he took over from his father. He does this for many people in the community. They pay him five cents per item. He does ours for free. His iron is constructed of heavy metal. I can't even lift it. He heats it in the fire. He has a big flat rock that he lays on each piece and irons it. He does this alongside the street.

Cars, carts, animals and motorcycles fly by, stirring up dust. I sometimes wonder why I wash the clothes only to have the dirt from the dust get ironed into the clothes.

Oh well . . .

Kites, Lights, and Lots of Celebrations

Our lives center around the Hindu festival calendar. When there is a festival, all offices and stores close and Papa gets to stay home. We usually go to a relative's house, or they come to ours and we celebrate.

Last year our teacher passed out a calendar with all the festivals listed. We have over fifty festivals in our Hindu traditions. There are hundreds of smaller ones in other villages. The big festivals usually last a week and are celebrated around a full moon. The rest either overlap or are celebrated another day. This means that the school calendar changes each year. Our teacher has to make sure we get our exams scheduled before the week-long festivals, even though most years the officials will change the exams, which messes up the school calendar anyway.

Most of the festivals are really fun. Our year starts off with Lohri. We get to stay home for a week and fly kites! We see hundreds of kites everywhere in the sky. Sumit is a good kite-flier. The boys have kite fights. They put razor sharp barbs on their kite strings and tails so they can cut the other person's kite strings. But it is not so much fun if you get caught in the razor string.

It is fun to watch. Everyone goes up on their roof-tops to fly their kites and to watch the kite fights. We eat sweets all week and the festival ends with a big gathering at the riverbank. We say our pujas, our prayers and chant. We end with a ritual washing in the river. I think it is supposed to take away all our bad sins.

In March, we celebrate Holi. This was always my favorite. Holi celebrates the triumph of good over evil because of the destruction of the demoness called Holika. There was an evil king long ago named Hiranyakashipu who thought he was immortal and wanted everyone to treat him like a god. Prahlad, his son, was devoted to Lord Krisha and refused to worship his father. That made Hiranyakashipu mad, of course. So, Hiranyakashipu demanded that Holika, his sister, burn Prahlad. It was thought that no fire would harm Holika so she decided to sit in the fire with Prahlad in her lap to keep him from running away. Holika was instantly burned to death but Prahlad was protected and survived because of his de-votion to Lord Vishnu. I think Prahlad became the new king, but I can't remember.

People all over India build 20-foot-tall paper mâché figures that resemble Holika and Hiranyakashipu. They are very mean-looking pieces. On the first night of the festival, we have a big bonfire and burn these evil demons made of the paper mâché. Then we gather around the fire praising Lord Krishna for conquering the evil with lots of singing and dancing. Everyone builds a bonfires, big and tall. It makes so much smoke it's difficult to breathe. I am always glad when this night is over because it can get very noisy and violent.

The next night we celebrate with colors. This is the fun night! We are thankful to Lord Krishna for the spring because of the food mother earth brings to us. The colors are supposed to bring positivity to our lives.

We gather in the streets. My papa holds me on his shoulders because he doesn't want me to get lost in the large crowd. So many people are all packed in together in the street. The drums start and we throw powdered colors on each other as we dance. I always laugh so much as I bop up and down on my dad's shoulders when he dances. Sometimes he will put me on the ground and dance, holding my hands.

Each color has a meaning. The most popular are blue for honoring Lord Krishna, green for rebirth and new beginnings, and red for marriage and fertility. By the end of the night a person is covered in many vibrant colors from head to toe. I never wear my favorite outfit since the color fades into the material and it is impossible to get it clean again.

The food during Holi is really good, too. Mam always makes *gujiya*, which is a sweet dumpling with dried fruits and milk. We also have lentil fritters that are drenched in fermented mustard water.

In the fall, sometime in September or October, we celebrate Diwali. I like this festival too, but it is quieter. Diwali is the festival of lights. As Hindus, we seem to always search for ways out of the darkness. During Diwali we celebrate "the inner light that protects people from spiritual darkness. "We take this celebration very seriously. It is a reminder to work very hard to make sure that we do all the right things so that the gods will favor us and give us a good, prosperous year, keep our families safe, and keep them from sickness or danger. We decorate our houses, and celebrate each other by giving gifts, especially jewelry. The festival lasts for five days and falls on a different day each year, depending on the Hindu calendar, again on a full moon.

Each day has a special significance.

The first day is called Dhanteras and is dedicated to the goddess Lakshmi. It is marked by cleaning the house and making *rangolis*, which are intricate colored patterns created on the floor with flowers, colored rice, or sand. People often go shopping on this day and buy gold because it is thought to bring good luck and prosperity for the coming year. They also make sweet and savory treats to share the rest of the week.

The second day is Chhoti Diwali, a day spent making final preparations for the celebrations. We offer prayers for the souls of our departed ancestors, and put out clay lamps, called *diya*, throughout our house, in every corner. We keep these lamps lit for the rest of the time of the festival. We also hang up string lights throughout the house and in our trees.

Diwali is the third and most important day of the celebration. Everyone dresses in new clothes and visits the temple to perform pujas. I always love putting on my prettiest saree and walking with my family. As we walk to the temple, other families join us. It is dark and we all carry our clay lamps. The scene is so beautiful with the lights sparkling in the darkness.

Typically there is a fireworks celebration in each community or village. And once it's dark, we light floating lanterns. It is a beautiful sight when hundreds of lanterns fill the sky! At the end of the evening, we gather around our table in the courtyard as a family, eat a large meal and play games well into the night.

The fourth day is called Annakut and marks the first day of the New Year. It is a time to give thanks for the past year, look ahead to the new year, and exchange gifts. In our family, we sit around the courtyard table and share the good things that have happened the previous year. Some people say pujas at their shrine, in their home or at the temple. We have a shrine with three gods. One is Ganesh, my papa's favorite god. This day is also dedicated to the bond between husbands and wives, recognizing the love between the gods Rama and Sita, the other two statues we worship. After bathing them in a milk bath, we dress them in their Diwali dress. Then we light incense around them and say our pujas. This is done to gain the favor of the gods for a prosperous year.

The final day is called Bhai Duj and celebrates the bond between sisters and brothers. My brothers, cousin, and I always spend this day together. We play games. We dress up in Mam and Papa's clothes, put lots of paint on our faces, and act out stories from the Vedas, our holy books. At the end of each play, we recite poems. Mam, Papa, Naniji and my aunties and uncles are always de-lighted with our performances.

We don't celebrate Christmas back in our village. We

know about it. The Christians who live nearby celebrate it. In Sumit's school, every December they celebrate Christmas. It sounds like fun.

Sumit told me they had a Christmas party. They sang songs, and one was called "Jingle Bells." He taught it to me so I can sing it with him. He says that they danced around a decorated tree and learned about Santa Claus—a man who is all dressed in red. He says this man flies all over the world and gives candy and toys but only to boys and girls who are good. He comes to their school every year. He is fat and has a big white beard. Sumit said that Santa gives them candy.

Santa doesn't come to our school. I guess we are not good girls and boys.

BOYS ARE BETTER

I learned very early that boys are better. I don't understand why. All I know is that boys get to go to school even when they are teenagers. Girls stop at fifth standard if they are lucky to get that far.

My brother doesn't have to do very many chores. Mam says that is because his wife and servants will take care of him. Until then, it is her job, and now, mine.

My brother also gets to go to school and finish the twelfth standard. From there, he will go to a university somewhere in India. I think those in the Brahmin caste go to England or the U.S. for university studies.

Men are the leaders. They are the mayors, police, government representatives, and prime minister. Indira Gandhi was a woman who was a prime minister; I have heard she was a very good lady. Not many women hold a political office.

Both men and women serve as teachers, but the women typically teach the lower grades, also called standards. Most of the business owners and workers in the stores are men.

Some, if they only have daughters, will let their daughters work with them. At least the Muslim people do.

But I can see in *The Times of India* newspaper that some changes are happening in the big cities. Some women run for public office and a few own businesses. And of course, some women are film stars. They look so beautiful on the posters on the buildings and trees in our village. Maybe one day I will get to see a movie.

But if you read *The Times of India* you see stories about baby girls being found in dumpsters or being dragged around by a pack of dogs. Many young girls are molested or killed and their attackers usually go free. If a girl is found in a hotel room with a boy of a different caste, her family will kill her because she has brought great shame on the family; the boy is either killed or beaten nearly to death. If it is not a caste issue, the boy goes home and marries someone else. The police and other officials do not get involved.

Last month in our village a young man named Udar let his wife die. An Indian cobra, a very venomous kind of snake called *naja naja*, slid into their home. Udar, only twenty-eight, was tired of his wife, Talika. He would complain about her to his family and friends very loudly. She would wash their clothes down at the river with us on Saturdays. I remember her being very sad.

On the Saturday after her funeral pyre was burned in the river, Talika's mother told us what happened. When the snake came into their home, Udar taunted it, picked it up with a stick and threw it on Talika. The snake bit her. She became very ill. The next day her mother visited her and saw how ill she was, but Udar was still making her fix his food and bring him his tea. He beat her because she was on her bed during the day. Her mother rushed in and was trying to take care of Talika, yelling at Udar to go and get the doctor. He refused. Udar tried to throw his mother-in-law out, hitting her. But she refused to leave her daughter. That night her daughter died.

Talika was from an affluent family, but Udar was a farmer. The women at the river say he killed her for her money. She had a large dowry worth 500,000 rupees[1], a car and some property.

Now he is fighting her family over the property. Unfortunately, in our village he will probably win. Talikah's father died so her mother is a widow. She didn't have any other children. So Talika's mother has no rights.

(Also, something to know about snakes in India. They are considered one of the Hindu gods. We do not kill them. If someone does kill a snake, they tell no one and in the dark of night, they take the dead snake out and dig a very deep hole and bury it so that no one knows they killed it. If they find out, the person can go to jail, or worse.)

I read an article in the newspaper the other day. It said that in 2020 the Supreme Court ruled that daughters have equal rights to Hindu family property. I think this means that all Hindu women now have equal rights to their father's property all the way back from 1956. That is when the succession law was first written. But in our village these laws are never enforced. I showed the article to Sumit. He just laughed. I don't think my brothers would ever give me any of our family property.

Even in the 21st century, boys are still better. And I still don't know why.

---

[1]   500,000 rupees is $7,000 US Dollars

Anrit, the Boy I Will Marry

When I was five, my mam, papa and Naniji went to talk with Anrit's father. Anrit is a boy who is seven years older than me. My papa set up a contract, offering a dowry of two cows, a gold necklace, and several chickens. That is what I am worth.

Anrit and I will marry when I am thirteen, or when I become a woman with the first blood. He will be twenty.

When a girl gets her first blood, the women give her a party.

A swing is decorated, and she sits on the swing, which is padded with many rags. There is singing and dancing. We paint our hands, arms, and feet with henna. And we eat fun cakes.

But after this party, the girl, now a woman, must sleep alone for a week on the veranda, or outside the house if there is no veranda. My mam even does this. We have a bed made out of bamboo with a tight rope stretched across in a checkered pattern. On top of that is a thin mattress. Mam puts rags down on the bed and every morning when she wakes up, there is blood all over the rags and soaked through the mattress. She takes those and washes them. The thin mattress has many bloodstains on it. She never washes the mattress. Then she sits the rest of the day on another batch of rags. That week, she doesn't have to do any cooking. She just rinses out the rags and hangs them to dry while sitting or sleeping on the other ones. The rags never get all the way clean. Neither does the one suit she wears during the week.

I am not sure I am excited about getting my first blood. From watching the women, it seems painful. And I don't want to sleep alone on the veranda.

The wedding happens a week after that party.

The girl leaves her family and goes to live with the boy and his parents.

The mother-in-law gets another helper. I hope his mother likes me so I will be able to sleep in the house and not outside on the front steps. I know that I will be the one cooking the meals, serving the chai, and cleaning the clothes. I think Anrit's family has a *dalit* who does most of the house cleaning because I see her sleeping on the back step every night.

I will also learn how to manage the daily worship of the gods. Anrit's mother will tutor me on which incense to burn for each ceremony, what chants to say, and which god they worship. Hopefully, it will be similar to what my mom has taught me. I must learn so that the gods will do me a favor and give me a boy for my first child.

I hope Anrit is nice to me. I've seen him kick dogs and beat the other animals that wander in the village. He's especially mean to his younger brother.

I am not so sure about this marriage.

But I don't have a choice.

The Baby Girl That Is No More

When I was eleven my mam had a baby. It was a little girl.

I was so excited to have a sister. Someone to share my doll with. Someone who can play girl things with me, and we could learn how to cook and clean together.

My mam was sad. So was my papa.

I asked my mam what her name was. She slapped me. Stunned and crying, I ran out of the room.

Going into Mam's bedroom, I go over to the crib. I pick up my sister and bounce her gently as I rub her back, like I have seen my mam and Naniji do so many times with other babies.

I whisper in her ear, "Ami. That is what I will call you. It means 'dearly loved.'"

I like holding my baby sister's hand. She wraps her tiny fingers around one of my fingers. My mam will not hold her. I don't understand why. I would sit with her, soothe and rock her.

I thought she must be hungry. I hope Mam will feed her soon.

Three days after she was born, I woke up, and my baby sister was gone. So were my parents. I hoped they would come back soon.

Mam and Papa came home. They did not have my baby sister with them.

I was so worried, wondering, "Where is she? She can't survive on her own. She needs Mam's milk."

I wondered, "Who is holding her, rocking her to sleep? Who is changing her diapers and washing her little body?"

Later that evening, I was laying on my mat trying to go to sleep. My little sister still was not back home. I heard the whispered voices of Mam and Naniji talking. Mam was crying softly.

"We went to White Temple. It was the time to sacrifice to Shiva. We walked the long steps to the very top to the old temple. The sacrifices began. It was painful to watch as they took my baby girl. I hope Shiva will bless me with a boy next year."

GETTING READY FOR MARRIAGE

I miss Ami so much. I don't ask about her anymore, but I still cry at night when I think about holding her and rocking her to sleep. My mam has stopped crying at night.

It's been a year since they took Ami away. Now I have a little brother. His name is Ashok. I hope they are allowed to keep him. Like my little sister, he wraps his tiny fingers around my one finger. Mam nurses him often.

Even though I am now only twelve, I no longer go to school. Mam told me that it is my duty to take care of my baby brother's every need, except feeding him. So, when she is finished feeding him, she thrusts him into my arms, and I bathe him and rock him to sleep. We do this routine several times a day.

I am now also responsible for cleaning the house and cooking the food. Mam is getting me ready for my marriage. These will be my duties. She no longer lets me read books. Sometimes I finish my chores quickly so I can sneak away and borrow one of my older brother's books to read.

I wish I could go to school. I miss my friends. But most of all I miss learning all about the world and the different places. I imagine getting on a boat and traveling to faraway places like England or America. I love to study science and learn about our bodies, but I like math even more. Taking numbers and calculating them, doing some equations—I find it fun to solve the problems and riddles.

But now all I do is wash clothes, cook meals, and take care of my baby brother. It's also my responsibility to take care of my older brother too. But I don't mind because he gives me candy and a book every now and then.

Is Papa Okay?

Papa works at a bank. He leaves for work at 7:00 am every morning and comes home at 6:00 pm in the evening. He is one of the clerks at the small office. He sits behind a glass partition. He has a machine that counts big stacks of money. He has to be very careful not to make any mistakes. He has a pad that has carbon paper in between two sheets. He writes down every transaction on that pad. Then he puts one sheet in a locked drawer, one sheet in a bag and gives one to the person getting or exchanging money. He works in the bank every day except Sunday, counting money and exchanging all the foreigner's bills to rupees.

Working ten hours a day, he eats his lunch at this desk. He never complains about the rats that run across his desk or around his feet. We have them in the house too, but we shoo them out. They could be our ancestors so we even leave a bowl of milk on the back step for them.

When he comes home, he likes to make wooden statues with his knife. He carves Ganesh and Hanuman the most. He gives these to his friends and to the priests. I think it helps his karma or maybe these gods smile on him for helping others by giving them a statute to pray to.

Tonight I was sitting in Papa's lap, and rubbing my hand against his arm. Papa has dark chocolate skin. It is smooth. His hands are strong. His hands are so much bigger than mine. I see a white patch that looks like a bandage. I touch it.

Whack. I am surprised by a slap from my papa that knocks me to the floor.

Papa is angry. I am crying because I don't know what I've done wrong.

Mam runs over. "Latika, naughty girl, what did you do to anger your papa?" She yanks me up hard and takes me to my room.

Alone in my room, I wonder what I did wrong. Later, Mam comes back and helps me to get ready for bed. She does not talk about what happened, and I know better than to ask because it will just mean another hard slap. She tucks me in, kisses my cheek, and tells me to stay away from Papa for a few days.

LEPER

I can hear her screaming.

I run from playing ball in the courtyard into the front room of our house.

My mam is still screaming, and she is on her knees, rocking back and forth.

My papa is standing there crying. It's the middle of the afternoon. Why is he home? Why is he crying?

My naniji is screaming at my mam and my papa. She is hitting them with the wicker broom and shouting, "Leper! Leper! Leper!"

The other family members run in. They start screaming too. Then they start running to our room and throwing out all our stuff.

Frightened and dazed, I wonder, *What is happening?*

WHERE DO WE GO?

My papa, mam, brothers, and I are standing out on the road.

Mam and Papa are picking up our belongings that Naniji and my aunties and uncles have thrown out of our house.

It's only a handful of clothes. We don't have any of our nice sarees or suits. We don't have any of our shoes except what we are wearing.

Mam manages to get some food and her wedding jewelry into a knapsack. Papa is stunned and just stands there. He seems confused, and I can tell he feels very hurt.

The neighbors in our village hear the racket. They are starting to gather around our house. Now, they are yelling at us. Some of them pick up big rocks and start throwing them at us.

I try to run to Naniji to hug her for comfort. She screams at me and pushes me away. She says she can't touch me because I am *achut*, untouchable. I don't understand. I don't have anything wrong with me.

I love her so much. I wonder, "Why can't she keep me?"

Mam grabs my hand and drags me with her. Papa and my brother follow. She thrusts my baby brother in my arms. I'm crying. She tells me to stop crying and to walk.

"Where are we going?" I ask.

No one answers me.

Walking On

Another village. They are all starting to look the same.

Camels pulling the carts loaded with long logs walk slowly through the streets. A man bathes in the village well. Another man sits in a barber chair outside under a tree while a man shaves his beard with a straight-edged razor.

Cows lumber down the street, dropping their paddies when they lift their tails. Monkeys scurry everywhere and try to steal the lunch of someone sitting by the road. Pigs root in the piles of trash.

Autos rush by and beep their horns. Motorbikes swerve in and out between the autos and tuk tuks. Many carts with big wheels are sitting by the road, full of fresh vegetables and fruit that cause my mouth to water and my stomach to grumble louder.

Children beg on street corners and run up to cars when they stop, knocking on the windows, begging for a coin or a piece of food. Shops are open, the owners sitting by the door waiting for customers and shooing the begging children away. The loud sounds of people, animals, automobiles is always the same in every village.

All the villages and cities smell the same. And why wouldn't they? Toilets are available but most people just *go* where they are. You will see a man peeing every fifty yards. Most will turn their back to the street; some do not bother. Women stretch out their skirts and squat. Many will have a small broom in their hand and pretend to be sweeping the street. They don't sweep away what is left behind when they stand up. Of course, there are the cows, pigs, camels, elephants, monkeys, rats, and other animals roaming the streets leaving behind their lunches and dinners too.

The first thing we do when we come to a new village is look for shelter. How I wish we could have a home like my naniji's. We see a huge cardboard box near a road that looks like someone vacated it. Papa and Mam go over and inspect it. It smells really awful, but at least it will keep us out the rain. We set up beside the busy roads. We do this because there are tigers and leopards throughout Rajasthan and staying beside a busy road helps provide some safety from these wild creatures.

Is This Our New Village?

We've been in six different villages since we left our home. Papa says we have walked over four hundred kilometers since leaving our village in Ved, Gujarat. It's been eight months.

I am hopeful each time we walk into a village. I hope that this will be the place we find a home and we stay. I especially hope we stay here in Planapur. I love the green grass and water everywhere. The air smells fresh, even though cow patties line most houses and fences. They stack them in huge bundles after they dry. They use them for burning and fuel. It just adds to the smells.

If I could get work in the field, maybe we would have enough food each day. They allow field workers to take a few squashes or fruit with them. If Mam works in the toilet, she will make enough to purchase grain. Then we could make *roti* and eat the squash. That would sustain us. I doubt I would be allowed to go to school but maybe my brothers could.

Planapur has many peacocks. I like it when I see a peacock. If it opens up its tail feathers to you, it is said that the gods have smiled upon you, and you will have good luck. I wish one would cross my path right now so our good luck could be that we stay in Planapur.

Mam and Papa get menial jobs as we go from village to village until the owners or bosses find out my papa has leprosy. Then the screaming starts, and rocks are thrown. We run. When we get to the outskirts of the village, we start walking . . . again.

Mam keeps saying this is our karma. I keep wondering, "I must have been a very bad girl in my past life to have to endure this now."

It's shameful living with a cardboard roof. We have no privacy. If I had clothes to change into it would be embarrassing. Of course, we can't take baths. We have no tub or running water. I usually go to the village well in whatever village we are in. I don't go early in the morning with the other women. Often, they find out who we are and will throw rocks or sticks at me. So, I go in the middle of the day when the cows and pigs do. It's hot and these animals go to the well to get in and roll around in the water. I wait until they are finished, then I fill our jug for the day.

We sleep on dirt floors. Mam and Papa take turns staying up at night to chase away the scorpions and poisonous spiders. Sometimes Papa has to chase a snake away. In the last village we stayed in, there were swarms of locusts for about a week. They were in our hair, our food, and all under our makeshift home.

I miss our home. It wasn't big compared to some, but

it was ours. My grandparents built the house and raised my papa and his brothers in that home. As their boys grew up and married, they added on rooms.

It had buildings in a U-shape around an outdoor courtyard. Mam and Papa and my brothers and I had our rooms to the left, Naniji and Grandpa had their rooms in the center, and my uncle and his family were on the right. Our *kitchen* was outside. Our oven was made in the ground. Our table was low, and we sat on the ground. It was easy for Mam to put fresh hot roti on the table, and even easier for us to snatch a piece off before the meal was finished cooking. There was a large swing and other sofa and chairs on the other side. We ate most of our meals in the courtyard, unless it rained, but where we lived it was arid and didn't rain much. I can't think of all those meals anymore. My stomach is growling too much.

When we were little, my brother and I slept in Mam and Papa's room. Mam and Papa had a big bed. Sometimes we would all pile in the bed together and Papa would tell stories. When we got bigger, my brothers and I had padded mats that we rolled out each night to sleep on. We each had a cubby that held our clothes. Mam and Papa had a closet where their clothes were hung on hangers. As we got older, Papa had a room built for my brothers and a separate one for me. We had our own rooms, even with our own beds! We each had a closet built into the wall, a desk and a chair. My room was my special place. I loved to open my closet and see my suits and sarees. I loved my desk. I had a lamp, my books and notebooks and a holder with a few pens. It was a treasure. I read my books and did my schoolwork at the desk. My desk was by the only window in my room. I could look out and see the small dirt hills and scrubby acacia trees. They look like mushrooms with leaves. They are not very tall. I supposed some people would call them shrubs. Sometimes I saw the camels wander over to the trees and eat the leaves. I liked to watch their lanky walk. I wondered if their necks would bend backward.

What I miss most of all is a warm blanket at night!

It has gotten cold and without a blanket sleeping is difficult. During the day we can stand close to our fire, but at night, there is no heat. My teeth chatter as I curl up in a ball and try to stay warm.

* * * * * * * * * * * * *

Mam came home today. She was kicked out of the toilets. I haven't been able to get work in the fields. Looks like we will be leaving Planapur and moving north.

Kali

We are walking again. It's a strange day, because usually we are walking alone. But today, hundreds of people are walking. Many are dressed in orange and white. My papa explains that these are followers of the goddess Kali. She was in some battle with Lord Vishnu and destroyed two demons. She is considered to be the master of death, time and change. Hindus worship her as the divine mother of the universe.

These people are very devoted. Once a year they have a celebration at the temple called Kalibari. To show their devotion, most of them will walk over seventy-five miles to the temple to worship her. But those who are very devoted *walk* to the temple in a very strange way. They lie face down in the dirt and stretch out their arms above their heads. They draw a line in the direction they are going to walk, then, get up and walk to the line, lay down and repeat the movements. They do this all the way to the temple.

If it would help me get food, or take away my papa's leprosy, I would crawl all the way in the dirt to the temple every day. But I'm not so sure doing any of these things would help. I've never seen any of the gods we worship do anything for me.

Maybe these followers just do this so that she won't destroy them.

I Wish

Before we were thrown out of our home I loved looking in my mam's closet. She had some of the most beautiful sarees and suits. She would get them out and show me the different stitching. My favorite was orange and red with beads and sparkling sequins. My suits, baggy pants and a long tunic, were also very colorful and had beads. Mam and Naniji made some of my clothes, but we also went to the tailors for our very nice pieces.

I loved going to the store where we would sit on very nice cushions. They would bring us tea. The shelves were full of individually wrapped ready-made Punjabi suits, each folded in a separate see-through bag. Sometimes we would buy these. But most of the time, the men would bring out different bundles of fabric. They would start opening each bundle and fluff them out in front of us. So many beautiful fabrics! Mam and Naniji touched them, but I was not allowed to. They discussed which ones they liked and asked the man, "How much?"

He told them a price and they shook their heads and

said, "Tish, Tish," clicking their tongues.

My mam said another price. The man shook his head. She raised her hands up and then he said, "Madam what do you think is fair? This is fine cloth, very good silk. We will make you the best saree in this fabric."

Mam said another price just a little higher than her previous offer, and he said okay. If he didn't, Mam and Naniji would leave, and usually, the man backed down and took their price.

* * * * * * * * * * * *

Now, Mam has to negotiate for work or a piece of bread. She barters and raises her voice. They call her names. It's not as nice as with the tailor-men. Sometimes, though, a few people will give her an extra piece of bread.

She only has the one saree she had on the day we left. It has small holes in it and most of the beads have fallen off. My suit is worn too, and I have grown a little, so the pants are too short. My ankles are showing and that is shameful.

I wish we could get a new suit. I wish my mam didn't have to work so hard for so little. I wish she could get a new saree.

But what good does it do to wish?

IN THE SHACK
BY THE ROAD

My father still doesn't look sick. He has more white patches, but he gets a cold or fever easily. It's probably because we live outside. Mam and Papa try to find some covering each night. Sometimes under a bridge. Sometimes under a tree with a large tarp. But most of the time we use another large cardboard box for a roof.

We have a fire going in front of our shelter all the time. My brothers and I gather as many twigs as we can. We also get paper from the dumpsters or anything that will burn. Many times we use dried cow chips, mostly that we have stolen from outside someone else's gate. We use a piece of cardboard to scoop as many cow chips as we can each day and take them to our *house*. We lay them in a pile to dry out. Once they dry, they make good fuel for the fire. It just doesn't smell so good.

One night Mam brought home enough grain to make roti. Since we don't have an oven, she cooked it over an open fire. She has a skillet someone left behind at another place we lived. She places the skillet on top of the fire because we don't have a grate or anything to hold it. It gets really hot. When she hands my papa his piece, he drops his roti into the fire. He sticks his hand in the fire to pick it up. It didn't hurt. He grabbed the skillet Mam used.

Smiling, he shows us his hand and says, "Look, it doesn't burn."

Mam scolds him and makes him drop the pan. He has burned his hand. Mammy bandages it as best she can. Papa still doesn't feel anything.

A few days later, the burned skin on Papa's fingers on his left hand is getting worse. We don't have any medicine to help make it better.

* * * * * * * * * * * *

For a few months we have been in this shack by the road. I am not sure where we are but there are more cars and people.

The tips of Papa's fingers are starting to fall off. Now, when we go to the village, Papa stays back and Mam and Sumit go to find work. Each day, I go to the village well and get water. Once a week, I wash our clothes in the well. Sometimes I have to wait for the cows to get out of the well so I can wash. If any of the other village women come by, they will not talk to me. It's lonely.

Papa says we are near Jaipur, the Pink City. I hear it is a big city. I wonder what it will be like.

Mam heard of a place we can go. It is a colony of lepers. There's no gate or fence. It is right by the city dump and in the middle of the big city. It will take two months or more to walk there. I will have another birthday before we arrive.

Arriving in Jaipur

We walked by a big palace today. It sits in the middle of a lake. There is no bridge to it. People walk along the bank of the lake and take pictures. It looks so tranquil and peaceful. A park area with marble stones and a statue of men playing instruments lines the bank. The men sell all kinds of pretty things, jewelry, statues, purses, and shoes from their carts in the park. Wooden carts are full of food, some already made and some they are cooking, which makes my stomach long for a good meal.

A man has a few camels and people are paying him to ride them. Another man has two elephants that are painted with beautiful bold colors and pretty designs. They have square saddles on their backs and people are paying to ride them too. It is all odd to me since back home we could ride these animals whenever we wanted to and we didn't have to pay. The camels are nasty creatures. They spit and they make a loud mournful sound. But the elephants are usually nice to ride, except the hair is so stiff it sticks in your legs and backside. Good thing they have a saddle.

After sitting on a bench in this area by the lake, Mam said it was time to go. We pick up our bags and keep walking. We walk under a big pink archway. We walk into a busy market area where all the buildings are pink.

Someone told us the palace ahead is the Wind Palace. We are now in the Pink City, which is the old part of Jaipur. All the buildings are made of pink sandstone. There are hundreds of people walking in the streets, more than I have seen in any place we have been.

The streets are narrow and full of cars, tuk tuks, camels pulling carts, food carts, dogs running in and out, people running in and out of the cars, and monkeys everywhere. Painted elephants are walking down the roads. Crossing the street is no easy thing to do. Cars don't stop for people. I watch as people walk in between cars, jumping to get out of the way when traffic moves again.

You have to be very careful when you drive in the streets here. It's not because of the people. It's their responsibility not to get hit. Of course, the cows amble down the middle of the roads just like they do back home. Many of them stand in the middle of the busy street just eating the trash. But you have to watch out for the holy cows. If you hit one the police will take you to jail. If the cow dies, you might die, too.

There are cow protectors in this part of Rajasthan. Once we were inside the gates of the Wind Palace, Papa picked a newspaper out of the trash bin. He read a story to us about a Muslim woman and her son. Some Hindus accused them of eating a cow. So, the cow protectors went and beat up both of them. The son died and the woman was severely injured, but it looks like she is going to live. After they did this awful thing, the police discovered that the carcass they found was not a cow. It turns out the Muslims had killed and eaten a goat.

The chief was quoted as saying, "Oh well. These things happen."

And in India, they do. All the time.

Papa finds two large cardboard pieces and sets up a little lean-to in the parking lot of the Wind Palace. This looks like it will be our home until we find the Leper Colony.

This parking lot has a water spigot. We use it each day to get our water for cooking and drinking. I watched a mother bathe her two young children in front of the spigot today. I am not sure they got that clean because the water is green and the dust turns into mud at their feet. But I am sure the coolness felt good.

Mam says we will stay here for a few days while she finds out more about the location of the Leper colony. I am kind of glad. My brother and I can play in the parking lot. And it is fun to watch the tourists. Women are in their beautiful colorful sarees and suits with their jewelry. They have rings on most of their fingers. Long necklaces along with their *mangal sutra*, which is the wedding necklace, hangs down the front. They have ten to twenty bangles, some on each arm. And they have rings on their toes! They look so regal and so beautiful. The men are in their long *kurtas*-shirts and pants. We don't see very many men in a lungee here, but every once in a while, I will see an older man with his lungee tied up between his legs.

Mam came back this evening. She says in a few days

we will walk to the Leper colony. It will take all day but she has secured a home for us. Finally, maybe we will have our kitchen and rooms and can get off of the dusty road. I hope we can have a bath!

GETTING TO THE
LEPER COLONY

Sumit and I scrounged in the dumpsters last night, fighting the pigs and the rats, and found a few pieces of leftover meals in white boxes that we could eat. Sumit has changed. He doesn't talk much anymore and he never wants to play games with me. He told me one night that he hopes Papa dies soon so he can go back home. Is that possible?

There is no chai or roti this morning. My stomach is grumbling.

This morning, we started walking early.

We walk for hours, stopping every so often to let my papa rest. Right after noon, we are walking down yet another busy street. A big shiny building that is all glass looms right ahead of us. The sun reflects off the mirror glass and I squint as I am walking. Big signs on the building are mostly in English. My papa tells us the signs say Prada, Louis Vuitton, Guess, and Cartier. I wonder what they mean. My parents do not know.

When we get to the building, we turn from it and walk under the overpass. We are walking down another road and pass an open market where a man has hundreds of shoes he is selling. I look down at my feet. They are dirty, caked with mud and by now have calluses. It would be nice to have a pair of shoes to protect my feet.

We turn again and walk down a desolate road. A few other people are on the road too. I see an opening. We walk through it and down another street with run-down buildings on each side. We walk a few more kilometers and there is an opening. To the left is a shed that has big kettles in the concrete area.

A man in a pink shirt, dirty pants and bare feet walks up to us. Mam tells us that he is the chief of the colony. He is clearly a leper because the tops of his fingers are missing just like Papa now. That is what leprosy does. It eats away at your fingers, ears and nose first. You lose your fingers. Your nose rots away, and so do your ears. I think this nasty demon then attacks your insides.

It seems the chief was expecting us. I didn't know it, but this is where my mam came a couple of days ago to meet with him and find out if we would be welcome. He takes us down the road. I see kids playing and running. Women are sitting on the steps. Men are gathered in a circle sitting on chairs or a cot with no mattress and drinking. We walk a little way, then he stops in front of one of the run-down buildings. He points toward the doorway, but there is no door.

Mam says, "This is our new home."

I run in, expecting to see several rooms and some

furniture. I want to pick out my room! There is only one room that is ten feet by twenty feet. A few rats run into the corner and crawl into a crack in the wall. There are no other rooms. There is no furniture except a bamboo cot with rope lattice across the top but no mat.

My mam walks in and I look at her and ask, "Where are the other rooms?"

She shrugs and says, "This is it. We will have to make this our home."

I am not sure what to do, so I just sit down on the hard concrete floor. I am tired. The tears start flowing but I try to stuff them down so I won't get slapped.

The chief man comes back after a few hours and tells us that there will be a meal given to us if we come down to the concrete area where the big kettles are. He tells us this food is clean and very good. He says it comes once a week just for those of us in the leper colony. Then he tells us to bring our own bowls. We have one bowl and a skillet. I hope we can get enough for all five of us because like every day, I am so hungry.

IN THE COLONY

When we first arrived at the Leper colony, Mam worked cleaning toilets, and Papa worked when he could. My brothers and I begged for food outside restaurants. We scrounged around in the dumpsters looking for food.

Sumit found some boys to hang out with and stopped helping us beg or find food. He kicked or hit me if I didn't give him my food at dinner every evening. It was easier to give him the food, and save a couple of bites for myself, than to deal with his blows.

Once he started hanging out with that gang of older boys, he was gone all day. When he came home late at night, he and Papa would fight. Papa always accused him of not giving him the money he made out on the streets. I am not sure what Sumit was doing to make money. His new friends are not very nice and one girl in the colony says that they sell drugs for a man who lives nearby. Maybe Sumit works with them.

Mam cleans toilets in a park. She makes 150 Rupees[2] a day. She also hands out paper wipes to the ladies who don't want to use their hand to wipe. Sometimes they give her a tip, maybe 10 rupees[3]. Since we are not allowed to go to school because my papa has leprosy, Mam brings me and my little brother, Ashok, and we sit while she works all day. Most days it smells bad.

Some of the stalls have these weird seats. My mam explains to me that those are called western toilets. India toilets are just a hole in the ground. There is a square plastic covering over it, a hole in the middle with two feet imprints on each side. You put your feet on each of the plastic feet and squat. There is also another nozzle beside the toilet that is used to wash your left hand after wiping and then to fill the bucket with water to wash down whatever you put in the toilet.

But these western toilets look like a throne with a hole in the seat. She let me try one once. It was strange.

When I turned fourteen, Mam told me to stay at home with my baby brother and take care of him and Papa. Some days she would send us out together and tell me to go to the street corners and beg for food. She told me to hold Ashok, or one of the younger babies who stay on the side of the road by themselves, as I begged because people would think he is my son and give me more money.

I was so hungry, and I didn't want to get beaten, so I did what she told me to do. On a good day, I would

---

[2]   At the time of this writing the exchange rate is 70 rupees per one dollar. 150 rupees is about $2
[3]   10 rupees is about 15 cents

get 70 rupees[4]. One day, I was standing on the corner at an intersection. My brother, now five, was standing there by me. A car stopped and my brother knocked on the man's window. He rolled it down part way and gave him a 10-rupee bill[5]. My brother was so excited, he stretched out the bill and was staring at it. Just then a boy, who was a few years older than Ashok, came and hit my brother in the face and knocked him down to the ground. The boy grabbed the rupee note and ran off laughing. My brother started crying. I just shook my head.

I thought, *He's going to have to learn how to live on the streets.*

Between what my mam makes and what we get begging, we bring home 1100-1500 rupees a week[6]. This is enough to get some good food. But Papa demands we give our money to him each day. He buys alcohol with most of the money leaving Mam with only 350 rupees[7] for food each week. We can get some vegetables from a street vendor who is kind to us. Sometimes we can get some clean grain to make roti.

Sumit only stayed with us for about a month in the colony. We only see him every once in a while. He gives Papa some money each time and stays for a cup of tea until they begin to argue. His visits have become less frequent.

But I don't miss him.

---

[4]   70 rupees is $1 US Dollar
[5]   10 rupees is about15 cents
[6]   1100-1500 rupees is $16-21 US Dollars
[7]   350 rupees is about $5 US Dollars

Bɑthing

What I wouldn't give for a nice hot bath right now. Or for someone to pick these itchy crawling lice out of my hair. Saturday was my favorite day back at our home. Especially during the hot summer months, because it was bathing day. We had water tanks in the ground at our house. I remember the water truck coming on Mondays to fill up the tanks. This was our water for the week.

We used this water to bathe, drink, wash some clothes, and for cooking.

When I was eight, Papa had a shower put in our bathroom. As I got older, I had to start taking showers. In our bathroom, there was no shower curtain like I have seen in magazines. We just stand under the shower nozzle to wash. Water gets all over the bathroom. We turn the water on and rinse our body. Then we turn the water off. We soap up. Then we turn the water on and wash off the soap. Then we turn the water off. We soap up our hair. Since mine is long it takes a while and in the winter months, it can get really cold being wet and standing in the wet room soaping up my hair. Then we turn the water back on and wash out the soap. Mam is always there and if I take too long, she turns off the water. We don't want to run out of water in our holding tanks. Sometimes I don't get all the soap out of my long black curly hair.

I wouldn't mind a soapy shower or a bath now. In the Leper Colony there is a communal spigot. We wash our plates after meals there. We wash our one set of clothes there. We get our water for cooking from this same spigot.

We don't bathe. Sometimes Mam will bring a bigger bowl in our room, and she will sponge me off. Now that I am fourteen, I do it myself.

I don't see my mam bathe. I know my brother and papa do not. The stench in our room is awful. But you get used to it after a while.

I never see the water trucks, so I am not sure where the water comes from or when they fill up the tanks. Sometimes the water is green and smells. Maybe, I don't really want to know.

THE DAY THAT
LIFE STOPPED

My mam comes home one day. She is bloody and beaten up. I don't know what happened to her, but after that she quits going outside the colony. I wonder how we will have any money to eat now.

A few days later I hear her talking to my papa.

She says, "No we can't do that to her."

But Papa is saying we have no other choice.

Papa calls me in from playing with my friends. On the cot that he sleeps on is a beautiful saree. He tells me that this saree is for me, and that Mam is going to dress me. He goes on to tell me that when I wear this saree, it will help us get the food we need.

I don't understand how wearing a saree can get money to help the family. But I am excited to bathe and get dressed up.

Mam brings in a big tub and fills it with warm water.

"Where did she get this big tub?" I wonder. It looks like she is crying, though she tries to hide it. But why would she be crying when I get to feel clean after so many months of being dirty? I don't understand it.

She bathes me and scrubs me hard. Then she takes some cooking coconut oil and combs it with her fingers through my hair. She braids my hair and puts some flowers in it.

Normally I would have a slip on. Mam always did. But I guess they could not afford one. We don't have any underwear anymore. I put on a short, cropped blouse that's a bit big for me since my breasts are just beginning to grow.

Mam starts the process of draping the elaborate saree around me. I remember watching as Naniji did this same thing to my mam. It was so mesmerizing to see the transformation of my mam as the layers of material wrapped around her body. It wraps around like a skirt, then she stops in the front and folds it several times to make pleats, she clips that part at the waist. She takes the left over part and drapes it over the blouse across my shoulder.

After she completes the process, she takes a black kohl stick and outlines my eyes. She does this to keep the evil spirits from entering my body. She takes some red powder and brushes it on my cheeks. Lastly, she uses a tube of red lipstick to color my lips.

I feel so grown up!

Papa comes in and inspects me. He is not smiling so I wonder if I look okay.

He turns to Mam, grunts and says, "It will have to do." He takes my hand and says, "Come."

I feel confused. He's half dragging me because I can't take big strides like he does in this tight saree. He takes me into a room. It's dark and takes a while for my eyes to adjust from the bright sunlight. I see a cot with stained sheets.

My papa turns to me. He says, "Mr. Prasad is coming in when I step out. I have arranged this, and he has paid me. You will sit on this cot, and you will do what he tells you to do. If you try to run, I will be outside and I will beat you if you do not do this. You understand?"

Now, I am shaking, tears are stinging my eyes, and I nod my head. I wonder, "What could he mean?"

Mr. Prasad comes in. He is a short, fat man. He sits by me on the bed. He smells of garlic and onions. I don't think he has had a bath in years. He tells me how nice I look. He starts to touch my arm and I flinch.

"Now, you are going to be a good girl, aren't you?" he says as he rubs his hands up my arms, licking his lips.

I am too afraid to say anything, and I just nod my head yes.

He slips the top part of the saree down and unbuttons my blouse. Now I am bare from the waist up. I shiver. He touches my breast and I want to pull away.

But he shoves me down on the bed. He pushes the saree up and somehow manages to take his pants down at the same time.

The next thing I feel is him on top of me and a shoot-ing pain between my legs as he shoves himself inside of me. The pain is unbearable. I scream and he slaps me hard. So, I stifle my scream because I know if I don't, he will beat me, or my papa will come in and beat me, too.

He is grunting and moving. Soon he is finished, and he tells me to get out. I try my best to cover myself. I walk out and my papa grabs me and half-drags me home.

He throws me into our house and tells Mam to clean me up. I am bleeding all over the saree. I wonder, "Will I die?"

My mam takes a wet cloth and washes me. She tells me to put my old clothes back on. She gives me rags and says to put them down on my mat. She takes the saree outside the house and washes it.

I lay down on my mat. I am still bleeding. I see the evil eye bracelet that I am still wearing. It didn't keep this evil away from me. I pull it off and throw it across the room.

As I drift off to sleep, I see my papa counting the money and telling my mom that doing this three times a week will be enough to get our food and she won't have to work anymore.

I can't stop crying. They have found a way to live, but my life has stopped.

A Puppet Show

When we first arrived in the Leper colony, a man and his wife came to visit. His name is Joshua and her name is Asha. We called him the Puppet Man. Together, they would tell stories and sing songs. It was fun to go and watch and to learn the songs. Some of the songs they taught us were in English.

I love when he brings puppets and does a puppet show. These are different than the wooden marionette puppets I have seen in other places. These look like the stuffed animals they sell on the side of the road, only much nicer. They are dogs and cats and funny-looking people with big heads. Their eyes are also big, and they look cuddly and cute. Instead of strings attached to a crossbar, the man and his wife put their hands inside the puppet and move their mouths. I love watching the puppets. They are funny. I wish I could have one to cuddle.

One day, I was dressed in my beautiful saree, which was not so beautiful now, with my makeup on. I was sitting under a tree waiting for the man my papa had scheduled for me. The puppet man approached me and asked if he could tell me a story. Some of the other kids were gathered around. He started telling us about a man named Jesus. He said this Jesus was walking down the road with a large crowd around him, and they stopped at a tree.

He looked up in the tree. There was a small man who had climbed up in the tree to get a glimpse of Jesus.

Jesus looked up in the tree and said to the man, "Your name is Zacchaeus."

The man was surprised that Jesus knew his name.

Jesus asked Zacchaeus to come down from the tree and said, "I want to go to your house right now for a meal."

Just at that moment, the man my papa had scheduled came up to me and reached for my hand.

I said to the puppet man, "Sir, will you wait a few minutes to tell the rest of the story. I will be back soon."

Joshua stopped. He looked at the man and he saw the way I was dressed. He put the puppet down and he said very softly, "Yes, of course I will wait."

I think I saw tears in his eyes.

By then, I was used to these men. They don't take very long and it doesn't hurt as much as it used to. So a few minutes later, I rushed back to the tree. Normally I would go home and clean up, take off my smeared makeup and change my clothes. But I wanted to hear the story. I wanted to know if Zacchaeus would take Jesus to his house, and I was curious what Jesus was going to do.

I ran back to the tree. I was happy to see that they were still there, and the man was talking to the children. When he saw me, he asked me if I was okay. I nodded.

He bowed his head for a few minutes. Then he gave me a sweet smile. It was not like the smiles these other men smile when they look at me.

He picked up the puppet and started the story again.

Joshua told us that Jesus is the son of God. In our Hindu religion, we worship a lot of gods. I wonder which god he is the son of. Then he goes on to tell that Zacchaeus was not a nice man. He was a tax collector, and he took lots of money from people. But Jesus wanted to eat with him. The people in the community were astonished because He would dare eat with such a dirty, mean man.

I am very dirty. I wondered if this Jesus would eat a meal with me.

THE COT IN THE ROAD

Now, on the day I wear the saree, my papa has pulled a cot outside our room on the street. He makes me sit at the end of the cot. Mam has gotten some cheap jewelry, bracelets, and earrings. She also found another saree in a dumpster and mended it to fit me.

In the evening around 5:00 pm, my mam makes me up with makeup and jewelry. And my papa makes me sit on the edge of the cot.

Men from the city always walk through the colony. Many are going to the big building across the street with the big signs in English to shop.

Papa always calls them over to look at me. He has draped a white cotton netting over the cot. At first, I thought it was to keep the mosquitos and bugs from bothering me. But I quickly learn that it is to cover these men while they have their fifteen minutes with me.

Most nights at least ten men pay to lay with me.

There's a young girl down the street whose father has

done the same thing with her. She is twelve. She has a baby boy. If it had been a girl, they would have put it in the dumpster or let the dogs drag it off. She told me that her papa told her that it was her fault that she got pregnant and now it is her responsibility to take care of the baby.

He said, "Maybe since it is a boy the gods will show you a little favor."

To keep the baby quiet, her papa gives her some of his opium and she rubs it on the baby's gums. She wraps him in a blanket and puts him in a basket under the cot while servicing the men. In between, she nurses the baby.

After seeing this baby, my papa warned me that it would be my fault if I got pregnant and gave me condoms. He told me that the men must wear them, and it was my responsibility to make them.

Looking at me with disgust he said, "The last thing we need is for you to get pregnant and have another mouth to feed."

I Want to Die

How can my father do this to me? I know I'm supposed to do everything my parents tell me to do and
if not, they beat me. But this?

Joshua talks about a loving father. I don't have a father
who loves me. I'm just a way for him to get money to get
his alcohol.

I wonder if I can just get away from all this.

Get away. Leave. Or . . .

I read about suicides in the newspaper every day. I
have nothing to live for. Maybe I can find some poison.
I read stories about people jumping in front of trains or
jumping off tall bridges into lakes or rivers. I could walk
to the railroad tracks and jump in front of a moving train.
There's no lake nearby or river to jump into to drown.

But if I do this I will just have to repeat my karmic
cycle over again. Is it worth it? Can I ever reach a better
place? Was I so bad in my past life that now I have to do
this?

Every night when I try to sleep, I hear voices in my

head. They are getting louder and screaming at me. I just want them to stop. They tell me how I will never make it to Heaven. I will never be good. I am dirty now. No one will ever want me.

I look in our cracked mirror. There are dark circles under my eyes. My hair is a mess. I'm getting skinnier every day.

I just want the voices to stop. I want the pain to stop. I want my life to stop.

THE MAN IN MY DREAM

Last night I had a dream, I think.

I heard a noise and looked up from my mat. I saw a man. I was scared.

"Oh no. Now Papa is bringing them into the house. Late at night. I can't do this!"

I pulled my thin threadbare blanket up to my face.

The man reached over and touched my shoulder. He said in such a gentle voice, "Latika, don't be scared. I'm not going to hurt you."

"I want you to trust Joshua. He will show you the way."

And then he disappeared.

I've never felt such peace wash over me.

But I lay there bewildered. What does this mean?

THE WHITE AMERICANS

O ne day, when I walked into the colony, I noticed a
very different-looking couple standing and talking
to our mayor. They are Americans. I have never seen white
people up close before.

The chief of the Leper Colony called me over to him
and told these Americans my name. The lady stooped
down to my level and looked me in the eye. No adult has
ever done that and I thought I must have done something
wrong. I stepped back, feeling a little uncomfortable. I
wondered what I could have done to upset her. I didn't
understand what she was saying to me.

I don't trust them. I have seen this before. People
come in who say they are going to help. They make a big
production of taking pictures with their iPhone. They stay
a few minutes and then they leave.

They don't stop to talk to us. They don't touch us. They
don't give us food or clothes. Most of the time they never
return.

Now, there is another man with the lady. It's the puppet

man, Joshua. He is the puppet man who was kind to me.

Joshua is speaking Hindi, so I understand him. He introduces me to the lady, Asha, his wife. Then, he turns and introduces me to the man and the woman. Their names are Mr. and Mrs. Powell. I call them Uncle and Auntie because that is what we call any man or woman who are adults.

Joshua tells me that they want to help us. He explains that they are the ones who provide the good food with chicken and protein that we get once a week. They are also the ones who give us clothing, shoes, and blankets at Christmas time.

Every week, on Saturdays, we get a clean meal. The meal usually has chicken and eggs in the curry. The rice is so white and clean. It tastes like Heaven. Joshua explains that we get this because these American people provide the money for the meal. Sometimes we get two meals like this a week.

Sometimes we get other meals or bags of rice. But it's not clean. There are bugs crawling in the rice. There is no protein. Usually, this comes from the government offices. It's never enough for the 750 people who live here in this Leper Colony.

Now as I look at the couple, I remember seeing them before. Auntie is tall and she had darker hair but now her hair is gray like Naniji. Uncle's hair is white, as white as his skin. He is shaking the mayor's hand. I have never seen a western person touch a leper, much less shake his hand and give him a hug.

I walk over to Auntie, and I grab her hand. She does not pull it back. Instead, she reaches for me and hugs me.

It made me think of Naniji. I miss her hugs. I haven't been hugged since we left our home.

Joshua goes on to explain that Auntie and Uncle want to continue to help us in many ways. He is talking about a teacher he has found and how they want to help the children in this colony learn to read, write and do math. They want to train them so they can go to a bigger city and get a job.

I think to myself, "Could that be true for me? No, it is probably just for the boys."

I thank them and I return to our house. It's time for me to gather the scraps I got in the dumpster today and make some kind of meal out of it with the wormy grain given to us by the government.

School Again

Joshua, the puppet man is back. He has another younger man with him.

He says, joyfully, "Hi Latika, so happy to see you. Are you having a good day?"

This is a day that I don't have to wear the saree, so I reply, "Yes, it is a good day."

Joshua introduces me to Deval, the man. He tells me that Deval will be the new teacher for us.

"Is it true that there will be a school?" I ask.

"Yes, it is, Latika."

"Can I come to the school?"

"We hope that your parents will allow you to come. We want to teach boys and girls how to read and write in Hindi and in English. We want to help you all so you can go and get a good job in a few years. Are your father or mother around? I would like to talk to them."

I take Joshua and Deval to our home. My papa sits outside on a cot. My mam is washing dishes in dirty water.

When Joshua told them about the school, he asked if

Ashok and I could attend.

At first my father said, "Yes of course Ashok needs to learn." Then he turned and glared at me and said, "But no, Latika has already had schooling. She has a job to do."

He needed me to *work* so that they could buy food. But Joshua talked to him again. He said that my schooling should not interfere with my work. Deval would teach the children from noon to 3:00 pm every day. We could do the homework in the evening.

Deval asks me and Mam if we could show him where another classmate lives. We walked down the street to Lina's house. I think he did this so Joshua could talk to my papa. I am not sure what he said to him but when we came home Papa changed his mind.

So now I get to go to school! It feels like I am starting over. My heart leaps for joy.

* * * * * * * * * * * * *

It was a few weeks before Joshua and Deval came back. But this time they gathered us around a tree. They had a stack of red notebooks, a bag of pencils and some books. There are 25 of us starting in the school. Most of the kids are under ten and this is their first time to go to school.

Five of us are older and have had some schooling, all to 5th standard. Ashok is starting with preschool because he has never been to school. He is smart, though, he will catch on quickly. As the eldest students, we will help the younger ones and also start with 6th standard. It has been so long since I have held a book, any book, in my hands

I am so excited to receive my first workbook.

Mr. Deval is nice. He starts by giving us a series of tests so he can determine the knowledge level each of us have. I am excited about doing math problems again. And of course, reading books! Mr. Deval told us that we can ask him questions any time. He says there are no stupid questions. And he doesn't even have a switch.

I think school will be more fun than before. I know I will get to learn so much more.

OUR OWN
SCHOOL ROOM

We have a building on the edge of the Leper Colony that the mayor found empty. It is large with concrete floors and open windows. The windows used to have a lattice woodwork in them but most have been broken out.

The building has a small courtyard with a concrete fence around it. Right behind it are tall buildings where normal people live. When they look out their windows, they can see down in the school room and the courtyard.

We started meeting there a few weeks ago. Before that, we met in someone's room or out in the street by the water spigot.

We don't have a door, desk, or chairs. We don't even have a blackboard. But Joshua says that we will soon. He has told Mr. and Mrs. Powell about the room. The chief has given this to us for school. We don't have to pay any rent. So Josuhua has asked the Powells if they know someone who can help provide the things we need.

Last week, the people who live on the other side started throwing rocks and cow dung into the windows. When we went into the courtyard for a break, they started throwing bigger rocks at us. This has continued every day. It doesn't do any good for the chief or Joshua to go and talk to them. They don't want us there.

They yell out things like, "You are too dumb to learn. Go beg on the streets, that is all you are good for."

And then the rocks start flying over the walls.

Even the people who cut through the streets of the colony to get to the mall or the train station, throw their trash at us. They don't want us here and they don't want us learning.

I always sit near Ashok and stay close to him in the courtyard. I shield him from the rocks and cow dung. Luckily no one has been hit too hard or hurt from the stones.

I hope we get some protection soon so that no one gets a rock to their head.

My First Christmas

We don't celebrate the festivals anymore.

Mam and Papa don't talk about the good things that happen each year. I know my naniji and family will not mention us since that will bring bad karma to mention a family member who has leprosy. I'm not so sure all these festivals and pujas and chanting have worked for us. Or maybe we didn't work hard enough in our family?

But now, what is there to celebrate? It doesn't seem that the gods hear our prayers. If they do, they don't seem to care. Maybe, I have sinned so badly that I can't be forgiven?

* * * * * * * * * * * *

Joshua is here at school today and says we are going to celebrate Christmas soon in the Leper Colony. He says that Mr. and Mrs. Powell will provide a delicious Christmas meal with sweets! It has been several years since I have had a sweet of any kind.

Joshua asks us if we know what Christmas is. My hand shoots up.

Before he calls on me I jump up and shout, "Yes, my eldest brother celebrated it in his school back home. He told me about how Santa visits the good girls and boys and gives them candy. Is Santa coming to visit us?" I ask in anticipation.

Joshua smiles and motions for me to sit down.

"Let me tell you about the first Christmas and why we celebrate it every year. Okay?"

Since we are sitting on the floor, we all start scooting closer so we can hear.

Joshua begins to tell the Christmas story. He tells us about a baby named Jesus who was born from a woman but he is God. An angel came to her and told her that she would have a son who would be the savior of the world.

I have often wondered where our gods, Shiva, Vishnu and Brahma have come from. It's a mystery that no priest has ever been able to explain. All they tell us is that they believe that god Shiva was not born from a human body. He was created automatically! He was there when there was nothing and He will remain even after everything is destroyed. He is lovingly referred to as the *Adi-Dev,* which means the "Oldest God of the Hindu mythology." And as to the other gods, no one knows where they came from, it seems that they just appeared.

Joshua goes on to explain that the mother's name was Mary and she was engaged to a man named Joseph. An angel visited Mary and told her that she would have a baby, not from Joseph, but from God. Mary was puzzled.

(I would be too! If I was pregnant before I married Anrit, he would have killed me.) For some reason, Mary and Joseph had to travel to Jerusalem. They were poor and had one donkey. By this time, Mary was very pregnant and rode on the donkey.

They could not have been that poor to have a donkey. I wish we had a donkey or some animal to ride on when we walked all those months to get to Jaipur.

Mary and Joseph get to Jerusalem, but there is no place available for them to go. Everyone is full up. Every house, every hotel. One of the hotel bosses has a stable where he has his goats, pigs, and cows. He tells them they can stay there.

I think to myself, "Even a stable would have been better than a cardboard box!"

That night, Jesus was born. Mary wrapped him in cloths and Joseph cleans out a manger, puts straw in it and that is the baby's crib.

Then, out in the fields there were many shepherds with their sheep. It was night so they were almost asleep. Suddenly they saw a bright light in the sky, which turned out to be hundreds of angels singing and praising God. The angels told them that the king Jesus had been born in Bethlehem, a city just outside of Jerusalem.

"Wow, this Jesus is a king?!" I wondered to myself.

These shepherds followed this bright light to a stable where Jesus was born. I don't remember but I am pretty sure all our Hindu gods were found in large palaces not dirty stables. I wonder if Joshua really thinks that Jesus is a god, much less a king?

Anyway, the story goes on to say that these shepherds

bowed down and worshiped this baby. Then Joshua told of some wise men from the east. I wonder if there were any from India. They saw the same star and followed it to the baby who was about three years old by the time they got there. These wise men worshiped the baby. Joshua said the baby wasn't living in a stable by the time the wise men got there.

So, this is Christmas that Joshua celebrates. A baby is born in a nasty smelly barn and His mother puts Him in a manger. It is sort of a miracle in that an angel tells her what will happen. And it does. Then, shepherds and wise men, the lowest people on the earth and the smartest people on the earth, come and worship Him as God. This is what Christian's celebrate at Christmas.

There's no big fat man in a red suit. There's no candy. Hmmm . . . Sumit's Christmas celebration sounds like a lot more fun.

Joshua tells us, "There is much more to this story, and I will tell you more as we get closer to the Christmas celebration. But I want you to pray. And you do not have to do this out loud. Our God hears your prayer that you can say to yourself in your heart. So, pray and ask Jesus to show Himself to you. He will!"

* * * * * * * * * * * * *

A few weeks later Joshua is back. He has two cars full of big bundles. He gets out of his car and he tells us that we will all eat together this evening. He has brought a special dinner for all of us.

Some of the people start to drag out tables and chairs.

They have experienced this before and they know what is coming. There is excitement.

I don't feel so excited. Where's the fat man who is happy and gives out candy? Will we get to dance and sing Jingle Bells?

We don't have a table or chairs, but we bring a big blanket and our bowls.

At 5:00 pm, Joshua calls people to start gathering. He says a prayer. He prays to Jesus and asks Him to bless this food that we are about to eat. He asks that God would be present tonight and that those here will know that this meal and the presents are from Him because He loves each of us.

"What?" I think to myself. "The meal is from Jesus, and we are getting presents?"

I'm pondering this shock when Joshua says that Jesus loves each of us. Again, I am overwhelmed with wonder about a God that loves each of us. This is so foreign to me and what I have been taught about gods. Will this Jesus show up here and maybe He will give us candy?

When he is finished, he tells us to sit at our place. This is unusual because we normally line up and they put the food in our bowls. But tonight, we sit and Joshua, Asha and two other people bring big bowls and serve the food to us. One person puts two sweets beside our food.

I pop one of the sweets in my mouth. My mam slaps my hand but then smiles. Oh, that sugary goodness. I haven't tasted it in so long. I think I will wrap the other one up and put it in my pocket for later. The rest of the meal is wonderfully good and so filling. We all sit and talk with our neighbors. As everyone is finishing, Joshua calls us to come over to the two cars.

He asks us to sit down. He then tells the Christmas story once again. But then he talks about how Jesus had come to the world and how He willingly left His home in Heaven and left behind all that he owned and the rights that He had. Joshua said Jesus chose to come to earth as a baby. I guess that would be like a Brahmin choosing to become a dalit. That would never happen. Joshua continued to tell us about Jesus and how he died a painful death on the cross. Joshua said that Jesus died for our sins!

I thought to myself, "If He died, He won't be showing up here tonight to give us candy."

This is a strange concept to me. In Hinduism, we have to work very hard, be very good and worship our gods many times a day in order to have our sins cleansed. Not to mention all the festivals where we do service or acts to the gods to cleanse our sins.

But then, Joshua tells us about Jesus rising from the dead. How can this be?

Joshua tells us that because he and his wife Asha and the Powells and many people in the United States who believe only in Jesus, that is why we received the beautiful meal and now tonight, we receive shoes and clothes. He tells us that they are the hands and feet of Jesus.

I look at my hands stretching them out in front of me. Wait, did I hear him right? Shoes and clothes? I can't remember the last time I had a new pair of shoes or a new suit.

I look down at my feet. They are calloused and dirty.

Then something amazing happens. Joshua's wife, Asha, brings a basin of water and sits it down beside me. She takes my foot and starts to wash it in the basin. Then she takes the other foot and washes it. I am overwhelmed. No one has ever gently washed any part of my body. And to wash my dirty feet, that is unheard of unless the person is an untouchable, Dalit. Asha is not.

After she washes them, Joshua comes up and gives me a bright orange box. I open it and inside are the prettiest shoes I have ever seen. I take them out and put them on my feet. They are a perfect fit!

I look up and Asha, Joshua and the two men are doing the same thing to everyone who is at the Christmas dinner. Tears are flowing down my face and down others' faces too. I look for my parents. My mam is smiling and has a pretty pair of purple shoes. Ashok is enamored with his colorful tennis shoes. My papa just looks with disgust, leans on his crutch and walks off to our home. No feet washed, no shoes. I see Joshua hand my mam a pair of men's shoes for Papa.

Thinking it is over, I start to stand up. Joshua then tells us that there are more presents but before he gives those out, he wants his wife to sing a Christmas song. He taught us this song in school, so he asked those of us who learned the song to come and stand with her and sing it. It is called *Silent Night.*

His wife has a lovely voice. It is so smooth and strong. She sings and urges us to sing with her. We do. Dusk has fallen and it has become unusually quiet. All you can hear is her beautiful voice as we sing with her about this baby who came to save us from our sins. By the end of the song, we are all standing with tears streaming down our faces.

When the song is through, it is very quiet.

Joshua steps up and starts to open some big bundles.

There are new clothes. He hands me a package that has a teal-colored new suit with beads! It has a peacock design, and the beads are different colors. It is the prettiest piece I have ever seen. I can't wait to try it on and wear it. The pants are long too. Now my ankles will be covered!

We sing a few more songs that we have been taught in our school. Joshua tells a few more stories from the Bible. People are starting to get sleepy. It is a late hour now and the sun has gone down. I am yawning. So, Joshua and Asha stand up and say goodbye.

I am so overcome that I grab both of them and hug them for a very long time.

As I walk back to our home, with new shoes on and a new suit to wear tomorrow, I can't help but think about this Jesus.

Can He really forgive all my sins? Does He know everything that I have done? If these gifts are from Him, does that mean He could love someone like me?

A PROMISE

My father has gotten worse. He has lost most of his fingers and toes. He stays drunk most days. Since he can't leave the house, I no longer have to spend time with men because he can't negotiate the deals. The old men still come to me anyway and try to force me to have sex with them. So far, I have been able to run away.

Now I clean toilets a couple days a week like my mam used to. It is stinky work, and as usual the rats are everywhere. But it is better than men laying on me and hurting me. When I get home from cleaning the toilets at the market today, I see Uncle and Auntie, the American couple, have come back. I run over to Auntie, and she hugs me. I stay right by her the entire time.

They tell us that they heard we were good students. They encourage us to continue our education, something I am very happy to do. They give us red spiral notebooks and I get my very own pencil.

Auntie sits down beside me. She asks me to write my name in the notebook. By now, I can understand some

English. I write my name.

She tells me that Latika means goddess. I don't feel like a goddess. She tells me that in God's eyes, I am valuable and that He loves me. I don't understand this. Maybe Joshua can explain this to me later.

She says she will be back in six months, and she wants to see how much more I have learned by then. She also has some friends in Mumbai who have a company and they hire young men and women when they finish 12th standard. She says that if I continue to improve, they will give me a place to live and send me to school to learn how to work with computers. She also says that they will have a job for me while I am learning.

It sounds nice, but I am too old now to believe every promise told to me.

But oh, if I could leave here and not have to be around these old men anymore, would that be Heaven?

QUESTIONS AND SUFFERING

Now, my mam has this terrible disease. She is still in the early stages. We know that there is medicine available to get rid of the disease, or to prevent it from spreading, but the government in our city will not allow the people to take it. Sometimes a clinic will deliver bandages and some topical medicine to soothe the painful sores, but not very often. They will not come into the colony like Auntie and Uncle do. They just leave the boxes at the entrance. I think they are afraid of catching the disease or affecting their karma. Most of the bandages are used over and over, without washing. Reminds me of our menstrual cloths.

I don't think my mam, who is a good Hindu, would take the medicine. She says that she has to suffer. It is her duty. No one in this colony takes the medicine. Like most good Hindus, they feel, just like my mom, that it is their duty to suffer.

Why is life so much about suffering?

If this God that Joshua talks about so much is so good and kind, then why are we suffering here? Why do my parents have leprosy? Will I get it? Why will He not heal them?

I am sometimes scared that those white patches will show up on my arm or leg.

I wish I could move my mam to another city where they would allow her treatment. Maybe someday soon.

I got a new job at a restaurant serving tea. I am happy, no more toilet cleaning! I still get to continue with school in the morning and I go to work in the afternoon and evening. At night they let me pick through all the scraps, so I can take dinner home to my mam and Ashok. I also get one free meal a day here. My papa still demands all the money, but I save a little back for myself each time. Hopefully, I can save some money so that I can leave before he tries to marry me to some boy in the colony. He doesn't have any dowry, or he would have sold me years ago.

I came home today, and he was laying in his own feces. I didn't know where my mam was. Ashok is out playing with some friends. I hope he hasn't seen Papa like this. I heat some water to clean his body. He moans, reaches for my hand and just holds it. I don't think he will live much longer.

ARE YOU REAL?

Today I am 17. Joshua is at our school in the Leper Colony.

He takes me and two other boys who are also 17. He wants to talk to us about Jesus.

I love to hear the stories about Jesus. He seems like such a kind man. Joshua tells us that Jesus is God. And I have accepted him as a god I follow.

Today, Joshua says, "I want to talk more about Jesus. I also have a gift for you." He handed each of us a Bible and said, "It's a Bible in Hindi so you can read it for yourself." I can't imagine such a gift. It is leather, not paper. He has written my name inside the front cover with a note. "Dear Latika, always remember how much Jesus loves you. He will never leave you. Only in Him will you find real peace. Love, Joshua." My heart is filled with joy as I read his note.

Joshua opens his Bible and tells us about how it is a book of stories that tell us about Jesus. He shows us about each of the books inside the Bible and he tells us to turn to the page that starts with the title John.

Then he reads from the book of John, "In the beginning was the word and the word was with God and the Word was God."

He stops reading, and explains, "Jesus is the Word. He is God. There is only one God. I know your parents and priests have told you about the many Hindu gods you worship but they are not real."

Then he said, "I want you to go now. Find a quiet place by yourself. I want you to read the book of John. Tomorrow I will come back, and we will discuss this more."

I found my favorite spot by the one tree in the colony. I was mesmerized by the words I read.

I thought to myself, "This Jesus is so kind. He is not like the gods I grew up with. They were mean and harsh. They were always ready to allow evil to happen to me. I had to constantly work to appease them. But this Jesus. He seems so kind. He says he doesn't want sacrifices. What is this?"

I dropped to the ground and said "Jesus, I don't know if you are real or not. I don't understand. But if you are God, the only God, and you are real, I want you."

I felt a peace rush over me. I have never felt this before. Could this be Him?

I fell asleep peacefully under the tree.

The next day, Joshua came back to our home.

He asks, "Latika, how did your time go with God yesterday?"

With a smile on my face, I said, "I found Jesus. I have peace."

A wide smile forms on Joshua's face. "Yes, and now

He will always be with you no matter what. Let's start to meet once a week and we will study the book of John. You continue to read it each day until I come back."

DEATH

My father died last night. I was laying on my mat and I heard his gurgling breathing. Then it just stopped. All I felt was relief.

When Hindus die, they are cremated. This is an extremely important ritual because they believe that the individual's spiritual essence will be released from their physical body so it can be reborn. If it is not done properly, within 24 hours of the last breath, it is thought that the soul will be disturbed and not find its way to its proper place in the afterlife. The soul will then come back and haunt living relatives.

The body is dressed in its wedding clothes including the person's jewelry and is covered in ghee. Then, it is wrapped in a shroud: men in white and women in orange. During this preparation of the body, scripture is read. Only family members who are Hindus are allowed to touch the body. It is believed that if a non-Hindu touches the body, the soul will not escape.

The body is placed on a bed made of bamboo shoots and marigold flowers of different colors are spread across the body. The oldest son, with shaved head, out of respect, leads the other men in the family carrying the body to the site for cremation. It takes three to four hours for the body to burn. We stand and wait until it is finished. Many times, the body will move, you will see the feet jerk or toes curl.

Fire is associated with purity and its power to scare away harmful ghosts, demons, and spirits. During the ritual the fire god Agni is asked to consume the physical body and create its essence in heaven in preparation for transmigration. The cremation is a sacrifice. The god Pushan is asked to accept the sacrifice and guide the soul to its proper place in the afterlife.

We won't have a cremation ritual for my papa. Lepers are not allowed to be cremated. But neither are holy men and people with smallpox. Also, children under two are not cremated because it is thought that their soul does not need purifying. They tie a weighted stone around the body and throw it in the middle of the Ganges or another sacred river. All rivers, it seems, are sacred in India. It costs $25 US dollars for each cremation, and we don't have that much money.

Sumit wouldn't shave his head and lead any ceremony. He is probably happy that Papa is dead if he even knows. Mam hasn't heard from him and doesn't know where he lives. Ashok is now eight and is sad. Now, since I am the eldest, I will not make him go out on the streets and beg any more. I can make enough money for our food serving chai. Someday, I will make sure Ashok gets out of the colony but not with bad boys like Sumit did.

Now that I am a Christian, I understand that all of this is not what really happens to us after death. I have been telling my mam about Jesus. I am glad that we can't cremate Papa because I think she would perform suttee, where the wife throws her body on the corpse as it is burning and dies with her husband.

In India it is difficult to be a widow, especially without any family. It is even more difficult to be a widow of a leper and have leprosy too. Widows can be thrown out on the streets by their families. No one cares for them. Now, I will take care of my mom and I will have more time to share this Good News with her.

Auntie and Uncle Are Back

It's March. Springtime. There's not much of a spring in India. We have winter and we have summer. Our winter is cold for us. In Jaipur, it drops to 9 degrees C (40 degrees F) at night and gets up to the high 20s C (80s F) during the day. In summer, it's over 37 C (100 F) degrees. Most days it's 46 C (115F) degrees during the day dropping to 35 C (95F) degrees at night.

Today I'm wrapped in a warm blanket that Auntie and Uncle gave us at Christmas. My toes were always cold in my flip flops but now they are better in my new shoes that cover my toes. But since I don't have any socks, my toes are still cold. People who come into the restaurant wear heavy fleece jackets. Many of the women also have scarves and gloves. For us, it is very cold. I wish I had a pair of socks for my cold toes.

It is also the day we get our wonderful meal. I practically run home from work because I am so excited to see

Joshua and Asha and to taste the delicious meal.

Rounding the corner where everyone is starting to gather, I see Auntie and Uncle. The chief and a few of the older men who are severely disfigured from leprosy, are chanting to them.

In Hindi they are loudly chanting, "Praise Father, Praise Son, Praise Mother Mary, Praise Uncle, Praise Sister" as they beat their tin bowls.

I don't think they know Jesus, but they are at least giving praise and thankfulness to God.

Auntie catches my eye and I hold my breath. It's been six months since I last saw her. I wonder if she will remember our conversation.

* * * * * * * * * * * * *

"Latika," Auntie calls to me, "I want to tell you something."

I walk over to her tentatively. I am always worried that I have done something wrong.

"I have a friend who owns an outsourcing company in Mumbai," she starts. "Do you know what that is?"

I shake my head, no.

"Well, it's a place where people in India talk to people in the US and help them solve a problem they may be having."

"With the computer skills you have learned, and now that your English has improved, I think when you turn eighteen next year, it would be good to see if you can go and work for this company. Would you like that?"

I say, "Yes, of course." Then I ask, "Would I be a chai

server?" because I am a little confused.

"No," she chuckles, "We want you to do something better than serving chai."

* * * * * * * * * * * * *

Now I am 18. I have thought about that conversation with Auntie over and over.

I have lots of questions. If I move to Mumbai, will my mam go with me? What will happen to Ashok? Who will take care of him? Where will I stay? Will I stay in another Leper Colony? How will I help people in the US since they are the ones helping us?

Maybe, just maybe, I would make enough money to go to a movie, just once!

Auntie walks over to me. Hugging me she says, "Latika, I have missed you! How are you doing?"

"I am very happy to see you Auntie," I say with a big smile. "Joshua taught me about Jesus, and I asked Him into my heart."

Auntie looks at me with her kind eyes and smiles a big smile, "I am so glad to hear this. He will always be by your side because He loves you so much."

I smile and nod my head, thinking how thankful I am to feel this love.

"Have you thought about what we talked about last time?" Auntie asks.

I nod my head, yes. But I want to tell her that it is all that I have been thinking about.

"Well, I have a job secured for you in Mumbai after graduation. You will work with a credit card company. They will train you in helping people with their accounts. It's not the kind of job you will want to do for the rest of your life, but it will give you some training and it will help you get out of the slums here in Jaipur. So, what do you think?"

I don't understand much of what she says but I am excited. "Will my mam and Ashok be able to go with me?"

"No, Latika, this is a job for young people. Your mother will need to stay here in the Leper Colony. I know Joshua and Asha will look out after her and Ashok, and you will have a phone so you will be able to call them as often as you want."

"You will live with several other girls in an apartment. And we have some friends, Joy and Pooja, who will also be able to help you get started. I think you will like it."

I am grateful and I am scared. I hug Auntie and tell her thank you so much.

GRADUATION

Asha brought me a beautiful white dress today. It has a long red sash that ties around my waist. I asked her what it was for.

She told me, "We are going to have a graduation for you and five others in the school. You will finish your 12th standard next month and take the final exams."

"We know you are going to pass because you are such a good student, so we are planning a graduation ceremony to honor you and the others."

"These dresses and pants and shirts for the boys have been given to us by Mr. and Mrs. Powell."

I am careful with my dress as I fold it up and wrap the red sash around it. I want to make sure I don't drop it in the dusty street or get it dirty.

* * * * * * * * * * * *

The day of graduation has arrived. As I prepare, I carefully put on my dress and wrap the red sash around my waist. This makes me feel so good inside to know that I have a new dress and that I have finished 12th standard.

I remember the day when I thought I would never be able to go back to school. I feel grateful that Jesus has given me His love. I whisper a prayer.

"Thank you, Jesus for your love and peace. Thank you for sending these people who care about us, even though we live in a Leper Colony."

The school room is decorated with colorful streamers and balloons. A table is set up front on a small platform. There are six chairs beside the table. There is a microphone on a stand and two big speakers on either side of the stage. Joshua instructs me and the four other graduates to go and sit in the chairs. It seems all the people from the Colony are gathering. Joshua instructs them to sit on the floor in front of the platform facing us. He then takes mam and Ashok and places them in the front row. The youngest kids from the school are all dressed ups and come and stand on the platform behind us.

Joshua calls for everyone to stop talking. He then says a sweet prayer. He asks God to watch over the five graduates as they start their new life. After he prays, he gives a speech about how important it is to get an education. He tells a few stories about each of us. He tells how each of us have new jobs outside of Jaipur. Like me, he and the Powells have found jobs for the other four boys outside of Jaipur.

Next, he looks back at the younger children and says, "It is time for you to do your part."

They walk around to the front of the stage. Ashok comes up from his seat and joins them. Deval starts the music. It is loud coming out of the speakers. The kids,

Ashok included, start doing a Bollywood dance! It is so much fun to watch them. They do another one and then everyone claps as they take seats beside their parents.

After the dance, Mr. Deval stands up. He has on a nice crisp clean shirt and tie and black pants. He talks about how rewarding it has been for him to be able to teach us these past two years. Then, Joshua stands beside him. He asks the graduates to please stand.

"First," Deval begins, "we have a very special award. This award is for a student who has received 100 percent on all her marks."

I start to blush because I realize it is me, since I am the only girl.

He goes on, "But not only that, she has worked hard to do more than a 12th standard student. And one day, I hope that she will be able to go to the university and continue her education. She is the brightest student in our school. Latika, please come forward and accept this special award."

I am shocked and too stunned to move. One of the guys in my class pushes me, so I move forward. Mr. Deval reaches out his hand and I take it. He walks me to the center stage. Joshua has a medal, and he puts it over my head. Tears are flowing down my cheeks. I am a girl. Girls don't get medals and awards, especially if there are boys in the class. Can this be real? I look at my mam. She is crying, too, but smiling big.

Mr. Deval motions for me to go back to my place with the boy. He walks over to the table where there is a stack of wrapped square gifts. He and Joshua stand side by side. Mr. Deval calls us one by one and we walk across the stage and receive one of the packages from Joshua. Then we stand in front of everyone and Mr Deval asks everyone to honor the graduating class of 2022 by clapping. All the people stand and clap so loudly. I think they are as proud as we are.

The graduation is over. I walk down and open my gift. It is a framed certificate. It has my name printed on it and says that I am a High School graduate. I give the frame to my mam. I can tell she is very proud.

On the Train to Mumbai

I am nervous. I fight back the tears. It has been a week since graduation. I thought this day would never come but it seems to happen too fast. I already miss Mam and Ashok.

I am sitting on the crowded train. Alone.

I am not really alone because the car I am in is packed with people and luggage. The train is crowded. All trains are crowded in India. The people sit when they can, most stand in the aisle and hang onto the rails. At the rush times, they are so crowded that some hang out the doors and stand on the side ladders. I don't see how they don't fall out when the trains are going full speed.

I have never been on a train before. I always saw the crowded trains when they would pass by our village, or as we walked down the dusty road on our way to Jaipur. I always thought how nice it would be to ride in one, just to give my tired feet a rest.

The benches are made of iron and wood. There's no padding so I keep moving my bottom back and forth to keep it from hurting. These benches were designed for two or maybe three people to sit on. There are five on my bench. Our knees are touching the people sitting facing us.

People are pushing to get into our car, standing in the aisle and several hanging right by and almost out of the door. There is no door that closes.

The windows have no glass, just bars down and across. I am thankful for that because once the train starts, the fresh air coming in will clear out all the body odors.

There's a mother beside me holding her baby, patting his back. The baby has soiled his diaper but the mother doesn't appear to be bothered to change it. Of course, the car stinks just like all of India.

I don't know anyone on this train. But I know that I am not alone. Jesus is with me. He walks with me every day now. I feel a peace I've never felt before. I know that Jesus will guide me and help me face whatever is ahead.

I also know that I have the support of Joshua, Asha, and Powell's, the white couple. Joshua and Asha brought me to the train station. I am starting a new life. Mrs. Powell found a job for me in Mumbai. It's a very big city and I don't know what to expect. I will be working in a call center. I have the skills to work on a computer and with people, based on the education I received at the school in the Leper Colony. This is better than serving chai. Auntie told me that this job is more challenging, and it pays better.

Joshua has arranged for a couple to pick me up at the train station in Mumbai. It is a husband, Joy, and his wife,

Pooja. They will let me stay with them for a little while. The call center has apartments for the people who work with them, but right now they are full. I have been talking to Joy and Pooja through *WhatsApp*. For my graduation, Mr. and Mrs. Powell, Uncle and Auntie gave me a phone. It's not a new phone, it is one of their old ones, but it works just fine, and I can't believe that I have a phone. It has the phone numbers for Joshua, Asha and Joy and Pooja. I was so surprised to get this treasure.

I will be on this train for eighteen hours. Joshua told me that I must keep my bags with me at all times. He said that people will try to steal them. I have a large bag that is between my legs and my big purse. Asha gave me some food. They told me that the train will stop in two cities for a long time. One of those is Planapur, the place I wished we could have called home. The other city will be Surat, but it will be an early morning stop. He said I can get off and go to the restroom but to take my bags with me. He also gave me 500 rupees[8] to get food at each stop.

He also warned me, "After dark, the train will stop several times in the night. Do not leave your seat. These are drug stops and bad things are going on. So, stay put."

The ticket cost 1500 rupees[9]. They didn't have enough to put me in a sleeper car so I will sit on the hard bench seat the entire way. Right now, I am sitting by the window. That is nice because it is hot, over 115 degrees, and with no glass pane I get a breeze. There is no air conditioning in this part of the train. We would all probably freeze if there were.

---

8   500 rupees is $7 US Dollars
9   1500 rupees is $21 US Dollars

I've been sitting here on this hard bench for four hours. I really need to go to the toilet and it doesn't appear that we are stopping soon. I ask the mother beside me if she will hold my seat, but not my bags. I remember Joshua's warning and take it with me.

The bathroom is an Indian bathroom and it is very small. It smells worse than the car. I balance my bag on the sink. As I squat over the hole, I look down. I can see the railroad tracks. Everything goes out through the hole down on the tracks. Maybe this is why back home in Veda, Mam warned us about playing on the railroad tracks. It's difficult to hold onto my bag, and keep my pants from getting wet with pee. But somehow I manage. I wash my hands and see the water trickle out the hole and onto the tracks as well.

The train starts to slow down. The man in the train uniform walks through and yells our stop. Planapur. This is one of the places it is safe for me to get out and stretch my legs.

Taking my bags with me, I walk out on the platform. There are people walking and running, it's so crowded. There are men with carts selling food and snacks. Walking over I buy a small rice snack and a Fanta Orange drink.

I sit down on the concrete bench and put my bags between my feet. I unwrap the rice ball and blow on it, take a bite. It is sweet with curry. I wash down the hot taste with my Fanta. I always loved Orange Fanta as a young girl.

When I finish the rice ball and drink, I walk around the platform for a little bit. I would like to get out of the train station and walk around Planapur. It is such a beautiful place and coming into the station I saw the lake and beautiful trees. But I am a little too scared to wander too far. I don't want to miss getting back on the train. I see a man peeing off the platform, kids running, playing tag, and the mothers taking a break sitting on the cold concrete floor. I think I will return so I can get my same seat by the window.

* * * * * * * * * * * *

I am dreaming about being in my home in our village. My naniji is cooking the most scrumptious smelling food. She walks toward me with a plate of steaming hot food.

Screech! Is my naniji screaming at me again telling me to go away?

I am startled awake by the sound. For a moment I am confused and not sure where I am. Then, as my achy body adjusts from leaning up against the window bars, I remember I am on a train.

It must be midnight. Everyone around me is sleeping. An old woman is leaning on the shoulder of her husband. He pats her hand as he adjusts slightly in his seat. Little children are packed on the floors and on top of each other. The man next to me is snoring and keeps leaning on me. I slowly nudge him the other way. He snorts and moves to the right.

I guess these people are used to riding in a train and all the strange noises. No one seems to wake up with the wheels screeching against the rails.

I am a little frightened, but I don't move. This must be one of those stops they told me about. I do as I was told, and I don't leave my seat. It would be impossible anyway to climb over the two men on the bench with me and step over all the people sprawled out on the floor.

Looking out the window, I see shadows. People are walking beside the tracks. I scoot down in my seat so that my face is not seen. What if they see me and take me?

I scoot even further down. I rearrange my jacket that I rolled up to use as my pillow up against the window. My eyes adjust to the dark night. The moon is even hiding.

I see men standing in a group, talking and passing things back and forth. One man lights a cigarette. They pass a bottle back and forth between them. They talk for 10-15 minutes. A scuffle starts but then someone yells from down the tracks. The little group breaks up. Some of the guys run out into the forest. One of the youngest guys jumps back on the train, thankfully not in my car.

The train starts up again with a jerk. People stir and adjust in their seats. A baby cries and his mother picks him up from the wicker basket and starts to breastfeed. She is rhythmically patting the baby's back. The sound of the wheels on the tracks and the hum of the wind in the window slowly lull me back to sleep.

THE TRAIN STOPS
IN MUMBAI

Arriving in Mumbai, I don't think I have ever seen so many people. I can barely walk off the train onto the platform. It is like a sea of people. I hear so many different languages that I haven't heard before. There are over 2,000 languages in India. The signs are in Hindi and English. I can read both now!

I am exhausted, and hungry after this 18-hour journey.

I wonder how I will find Joy and Pooja. I am just following the people who seem to be going to a building. That must be the way out. Although some people are running to catch other trains.

As I walk out of the platform and into the building, I see lots of people with signs. I start looking. The signs have names on them. I finally see a kind young man with a sign that has my name. A beautiful young pregnant woman stands next to him. We recognize each other from our *WhatsApp* video chats. I wave and they smile at me.

They look kind.

Joy asks, "Latika, are you hungry?"

"Yes," I am almost in tears, "I haven't eaten anything in the last twelve hours."

They take me to a nearby restaurant. I've never been in one. I am not sure what to do. Someone hands me a piece of paper. There is a list of food with prices. It looks very expensive. Joy asks if he can order for me. I just nod my head because I am not sure what he means.

The man comes back. He has a small writing pad in his hand, and he takes the pencil out from behind his ear. Joy tells him the food that he wants. He orders garlic butter naan, chicken tikka masala, basmati rice, paneer, and lassi. I cannot remember the last time I had lassi.

The food was so good. It brought back memories of Naniji and her cooking. It must have cost a fortune because Joy paid a 1,000 rupee[10] bill for all three of our meals and told the waiter to keep the change.

When we leave the restaurant, Joy drives us to their home. He has a small car, and I am sitting in the front seat beside him. I've never ridden in a car before. It's scary. I have watched the crazy driving in Jaipur before but being in the car is even more scary. And in Mumbai, there are more people, more cars, more carts, more animals, and more motorcycles in the road than I have ever seen. Everyone just seems to go wherever they want.

We stop at a light. A car pulls up and stops his bumper right next to my door. The driver blows his horn. Apparently, we are in his way. We can't move out of his way

---

[10]   1000 rupees is $14 US Dollars

because there are cars on every side of us. The man gets out of his car and starts yelling at Joy. He says that Joy hit him. Joy calmly gets out of the car. He walks to the front of the car and this older man runs up to him and slaps him. Pooja and I gasp. I want to get out of the car and defend Joy but Pooja tells me to sit very still and not to get out of the car. She explains that could cause others to get out of their cars and a riot would start, and I would get hurt.

Joy just stands there. The man slaps him again on the other cheek. He yells some words at Joy that I don't understand. Then he gets back into his car. Joy comes back to the car. He explains that he said to the man kindly that he didn't hit him but that he would be glad to follow him to the police station. After the man hit him, Joy just turned his face so that the man could hit him again. The man yells things that were not nice to Joy and just leaves. I guess we are okay now.

It takes over an hour to drive fifteen miles to Joy and Pooja's house. By the time we arrive, I am very sleepy and tired. We walk into the front door and there is a room with a couch and some chairs. Another opening leads to a room with a sink and a table with six chairs. I know this is a dining room but I have never seen one before. We always ate in our courtyard on the ground around a low table.

Pooja shows me their bedroom to the left with a nice bathroom and one of those western toilets. Then she takes me to the kitchen in the back of the house. I have never seen a kitchen inside a house before either. I see shiny things that I have also never seen before. She explains that those are a stove top where she boils water and cooks food, a refrigerator to store food, and a toaster that makes bread. All these features in the house are new and strange to me. I see a black box with a window that she calls a microwave. She explains that the large white container on the cabinet is a water filter. It has a long hose that goes out the window to a big tank. She says that the water man comes once a week and fills up the big tank. It will be enough for cooking, washing, and cleaning.

Then she takes me to the left side of the house to another room. It has a built-in closet, bed, a desk and a chair. I see a water bottle and several books on a small table by the bed. She shows me another bathroom that is connected to this room with a western toilet. Pooja explains that this will be my room while I stay with them. I start to cry a little. It reminds me of my room as a little girl.

It's very hot and Pooja turns on a white long thing that hangs from the top of the wall. It blows cool air. So nice.

Pooja tells me to rest. She knows I am sleepy and says we can unpack after my nap.

She leaves and I lay down on the bed. It is so comfortable. I can't remember what my old bed felt like. But this is a soft mattress and the blanket smells so nice. I quickly drift off to sleep.

WORKING IN MUMBAI

Work is difficult at first. I sit at a desk, surrounded by other people at their desks. I have a computer, a phone, and a headset. There is a small wall between me and the other people working at their desks.

I work for an outsourcing company that handles new accounts for a credit card company.

I didn't know what a credit card was but learned all about debit and credit cards in my two-week training class. My job is to answer the phone when it rings, and it rings all the time. I work with the person calling to help them with their problems on their account. Sometimes I have to take their payment. Sometimes I help them troubleshoot on their account and their app. If it gets too technical, I have to transfer them to someone who knows more about computers and apps than I do.

It's a difficult job. Most of the people I talk to on the phone are from different countries. They have a hard time understanding me, and I can't understand them either. Sometimes they get angry and I understand their frustration.

Some are very kind and that makes it a good day.

I get a break for lunch, and I get two short breaks, one in the morning and one in the afternoon. I start work at 8:00 am in the morning and work until 8:00 pm at night. Once I learn everything, they will shift me from 8:00 pm to 8:00 am. That is when we get the most calls since we handle calls from the United States, England and Australia, the English-speaking countries. I bring my lunch in a tin holder. At the breaks we are served chai, and the chai server also brings us chai during the day. I am glad that I was able to get a job at this desk instead of serving chai like back home.

Everyone treats the chai server so badly. Most of them are Dalits, the lowest caste in Hindu culture. They are known as the *untouchable* and not thought of as a real people. But I know they are and that Jesus loves them so I try to be kind to them.

The four main castes in the Hindu system are Brahmin, Kshatriyas, Vaishyas and Shudras. Hindus believe that these castes came from Brahma, the Hindu god of creation. The Brahmins are mainly teachers and intellectuals believed to have come from Brahma's head. The Kshatriyas, or the warriors and rulers, supposedly came from his arms. The third slot went to the Vaishyas, or the traders, who were created from his thighs. At the bottom of the heap were the Shudras, who came from Brahma's feet and did all the menial jobs.

My family were Kshatriyas. If my papa had not gotten leprosy, we would have been well-respected and treated kindly. People know your caste. You don't have to tell them, although it is written on your identity card. If the people at my job knew that my papa was a leper, I don't think I would be allowed to work here.

I've tried to meet some of the girls and guys who do the same work. They already have their group of friends. It seems like they go together after work and eat together. They talk about dancing and drinking a lot. They also go to movies and talk about the people in the movies as if they know them. I would like to go to a movie someday. I have heard of them but never had the money to go to one.

These people also talk about dating. That is a strange concept to me. We have arranged marriages in India. The boy or girl trusts their parents to choose the right mate for them. It seems to work since no one talks much about getting divorced.

I don't understand how a boy and a girl can go on a date. And I certainly would not go with a boy by myself. I think I would need a parent or another adult in the room with us. Now that my papa has died, I hope that Joshua will arrange my marriage in a few years. But I have no dowry, and I am not sure how it works now that I am a Christian.

Sapna, one girl with very long beautiful straight black hair, talks about her boyfriends. She says she wants to enjoy this time now before her parents arrange her marriage. She leaves work with a different guy every day, it seems. It is all that the girls talk about, except for clothes, purses, shoes, and jewelry.

When I leave work, I take a tuk tuk to Joy's church each evening. We have a time of praise and worship. I enjoy these times. I have met a few ladies at church. We pray together every day, and they encourage me to reach out to the girls at work. I am glad I have this small group of friends.

Soon I will move to my own flat with eight other girls from work. We had to wait until one came available and they told us this week that it should be ready in another week.

I've been to the apartment building and have seen what our flat will look like. The building is very tall with over thirty floors and surrounded by other buildings with that many or more floors. Each flat has a balcony and you can see laundry hanging from the railing. It looks like some people try to grow herbs or other plants, but I am not sure the balcony is the right environment because the plants look pretty sickly.

The flat is laid out like Joy and Pooja's house, only smaller. There are two bedrooms so I will share with three of the other girls. It has the air conditioner, stove top, refrigerator, and a toaster too. It has one bathroom. I will miss Joy and Pooja. They have been so kind.

Also, the building is not very close to the church. I don't think I will be able to go there every evening but, hopefully, I will be able to take a tuk tuk and go on Sunday.

GIRL TALK

We moved into our apartment on a Friday after work. I didn't have much to move in, just my few clothes.

I have eight roommates. The three who are in my room are Sapna, the girl who is obsessed with boys, Pria who is from Kerala, and Binita who doesn't fit the meaning of her name, which is modest. They all had things they brought with them like lamps, rugs, pillows, bed sheets, cooking utensils and pictures for the wall. No one brought a statue of their god. They all have a lot of clothes and shoes. I notice that they wear a different outfit to work each day. I have two. I wear one all week and then wear the other the next week. Joy and Pooja gave me a set of bedsheets, a blanket and a reading lamp. It was nice to have something to put in my room that was mine.

Pria is nice. She is from the south, so the other two girls don't really care for her. She wears the traditional Punjabi suit, like I do. But she is more modern than me. She and I share a bed. She is not very clean though. Her clothes are all over the floor and she leaves dirty dishes on her bedside table. I don't know if she expects me to pick up after her.

Sapna and Binita are very different from any girls I have known. They must be like the women in the movies or TV shows. They wear jeans and cropped shirts. They even wear shirts that do not have any sleeves. And on Saturdays or holidays, they wear shorts. I had never heard of those until I came here to work. These pants are cut off and they show their entire legs. They leave the apartment like that. I would be ashamed to leave the house with my legs and arms showing. There is no modesty with either girl.

After we moved in on Friday, we took our chairs out on the balcony. I fixed some chai and brought out the tray with eight cups. The other girls looked at each other and started laughing. Then Binita held up a large colorful bottle. Sapna pulled out hers and they clinked them together. The bottles had a gold color liquid in them.

Sapna took the chai cups and filled them with the liquid.

She gave one to me and said, "Don't drink it down like tea, just take a little sip. It will warm you all over."

Sniffing it, I didn't like the smell. I knew what it was. It was the same thing that my papa and those other men smelled like. I just held it for a little bit.

The other girls took their cups and filled them up. Sapna popped her head back and drank her cup. Binita and Pria just took sips. They all looked at me and laughed.

"Did you see the new dude that came in today?" asked Binita. "He looks so fine in that slim cut purple shirt. Did anyone get his name?"

"Yes, it's Gyan and he's spoken-for, girls!" squealed

Sapna. "He's mine and you can't have him."

"Oh," I asked, "Is he your husband? Are you betrothed? When is your wedding?"

The girls just looked at each other and broke out laughing.

Pouring another cup of whisky, Sapna just shook her head, "No. Are you kidding? My parents haven't made my match yet. I don't want to get married until I am thirty."

"You see little Latika, I want to be with as many men as I can before I have to settle for just one. Besides, it's fun. Why should a man get all the fun? Right girls?"

I wonder what is so fun about sex.

PERIOD

I started my period today. I wonder if the other girls get their period. They never stay home from work and I never see their rags. I wonder where I am supposed to sleep. I think I can talk to Pria about this. She doesn't laugh at me when we are alone in our room, and I have other questions.

"Pria," I say tentatively, "I started my period. So, I guess I won't be going to work today."

She looks at me quizzically. "Latika, you must go. I know you are from a village, but women do not stay home in the city just because they have their periods."

"But what will I do? I have my rags and I am not sure where I am supposed to sit and sleep? How can I go to work and get blood everywhere?"

"Do you not know about pads?"

"What are pads?" I ask.

"Oh girl. I guess you never saw *Pad Man*. Gee, village women in India are so backward."

She goes over to her dresser and pulls out a square

package.

"Here," she says, "Put this in your panties and here's another one for this afternoon. After work, I will take you to the pharmacy and we will get you your own."

I open the package and fold out the pad. It looks very strange.

"Just pull off that strip and push in on the panty. It has sticky stuff that will stay on your panty. The pad will soak up the blood and not get on your clothes. When it gets full, go and change it with the other pad. Tonight, you will wear one and just sleep in your bed. If it leaks, just wash your sheets. You have an extra set, right?"

I just stare at this little strip she calls a pad and wonder, "How in the world does it hold that much blood?"

"And hurry up. We need to leave for work in ten."

* * * * * * * * * * * * *

It's been uncomfortable. But this pad does seem better than sitting on rags all day.

Pria pops her head over my cubicle wall, "How's it going? Everything okay?"

I am on a call, so I shake my head sideways like we do in India.

"I will wait for you to get through, then let's go on a chai break."

I hold up my finger and mouth, "Just a minute."

"Okay Mrs. Wright. I am so glad you got it to work. I know you will enjoy all the benefits that this card has to offer. If you will stay on the line, there is a survey you can fill out about how I have helped you today. Have a great day."

"Latika, get the other pad and hide it in your hand. Come on, let's go."

Pria practically pulls me out of my cubicle. She drags me into the bathroom first.

"Turn around, let's just make sure you didn't leak."

She inspects my back side, as I lift up my Kurta. "You're all good. Now go change the pad out. Roll toilet paper around the used one and put it in the trash beside the toilet. You don't flush pads."

After I come out of the stall, we go and get a chai.

"Latika, you are going to be a westernized, sophisticated Indian woman soon!"

She says it like it is a good thing. I am not so sure it is.

Bollywood and
Going Out

A couple of months later, we were all sitting on the balcony again.

"Latika, have you seen the movie *Queen*? I want to be Vijayalakshmi from that movie . . . you could be Rani!" Sapna starts giggling.

By now she's had half of a bottle of whiskey by herself.

"I don't know what you are talking about. I have never been to a movie."

"OOOOOH," squeals Binita. "We've got to take you to a movie right now."

"I love Rajkummar! He was in *Queen*. He has a new one out called *Hum Do Hamare Do*. Let's go see it. I will look it up."

"Get dressed girls, we are going out!"

Binita comes out of our room. I thought she would change out of her shorts but instead she has them on. She added a long drape with lots of fringe, a long necklace and an armful of bangles. She put on high heel boots.

Sapna is wearing the tightest pair of jeans that I have seen yet. It's like she has melted into them. Instead of a long kurta, she has a cropped top. She too has several long necklaces and is wearing bangles on both arms. She's wearing high heeled shoes. She has dark eyeliner around her eyes and bright red lipstick. The memory of having my face made up for one of those men makes my stomach lurch.

Pria is in a punjabi suit that is very colorful. Hers is more modest but the kurta is tight to her breast. Her makeup and jewelry looks like the others.

I look at my brown kurta and my tan pants. The girls look at me.

"No," says Binita, "This won't do. Girl, don't you have something sexier to wear?"

I just shake my head no. I don't want to be sexy. I don't want to dress like them.

But Sapna isn't taking *no* for an answer.

She drags me to her room. She pulls out a kurta suit, thank goodness. It is red and yellow with beads all over it. I take off my suit and slip on the kurta. It is kind of tight but it is really pretty. I put on the pants and Sapna sits me on her bed. She starts to apply makeup and I try to protest.

She says, "This will be fun, I won't put too much on."

I give her a *not so sure I trust you* look. She wants me to wear lipstick, but I refuse. I will not ever wear lipstick again.

Binita brings some high heels, but I can't walk in them, so she gives me some beaded sandals.

I guess I am ready. I am going to my first movie. That

makes me a little excited.

* * * * * * * * * * * *

Wow. The movie was like nothing I imagined.

And so were my roommates.

Sapna had texted Gyan. He was at the theater when we arrived.

We purchased our tickets outside the door, then we walked into a big area. People were just standing around. Pria took me to the counter. She ordered a coke and popcorn for me. I had never had either. The other girls got the same.

We walk into the theater. Sapna is hanging on Gyan's arm. She waves to us, and they walk up to the top of the rows of seats and sit down in the middle.

Pria follows them, so I follow her. When we sit down, Binita pulls out a silver square container with a twist top.

She opens it and says, "Give me your coke."

I hand it to her, and she pours some liquid in it. It was clear and didn't smell. I asked her what it was, and she said to just drink it; it would make the movie much better. She also filled up Pria's and Sapna's cups. Gyan had his own silver container and was drinking straight from it.

I take a sip of my coke. It has a strange tangy taste. I take another drink. This is the first time I have had coke and popcorn. I like the salty taste of the popcorn, and the coke is unusual.

I am feeling warm inside. A huge white screen is in front of us. I jump when the light goes out and almost spill my coke. And the movie starts with loud music.

I am mesmerized by the movie. The actors look larger

than life. The scenes are so beautiful. Wherever they filmed this doesn't look like any city in India that I have been to. There are no dirty crowded roads, no dust in the houses. And all the people in every scene are dressed in beautiful outfits. It is all too clean.

About halfway through I look over at Sapna. She and Gyan are kissing and grabbing each other. I quickly turn back to watch the movie. I can't believe that she is letting him do that to her. I don't understand why.

I finish my popcorn about halfway through the movie. I don't finish my coke because I realize Binita put alcohol into it. But it didn't smell.

She whispered, "Vodka," when I kept smelling it.

I was feeling strangely calm and so I stopped drinking it.

After the movie Sapna said, "Let's go dancing!"

Everyone shouts yes and I just go with them.

We walk down the street to another building that has lights around the door. The door is painted red. We walk in. People are standing wall to wall. We push our way through and in the middle of this room people are dancing. The music is loud.

Binita shouts, "Latika, grab that table and I'll go get us a coke," she winked.

"Just coke!" I demanded.

I sit at the table. Sapna and Gyan go out dancing with the others. He is holding her close, and she is rubbing her body up and down his. I turn away blushing.

Pria sits with me. "Do you like to dance?" she asked.

"I've only danced with my family at festivals. I don't know how to do this."

Binita comes back and says, "drink your coke and then we will go teach you this dance."

I take a sip, tentatively. It tastes like the other coke, and I don't feel anything. So, I drink some more.

"Thanks for not putting any alcohol in this drink," I say to Binita.

She looks at Pria and smiles.

After we finish our cokes, they drag me out on the dance floor.

Wow, the lights seem to be pulsing through my body and the beat of the music is ringing in my head. I can feel it. The music seems to be moving my body. I watch the other girls and mimic their motions.

We dance for what seems like hours. It was exhilarating. Binita brought another coke for us. I drank this one faster because I was so thirsty. And we kept dancing.

Then some guys come up and start dancing with us. One guy grabs me around the waist. It felt nice but scary at the same time. He started dancing with me. Then, he reached down, I think to kiss me.

I pulled back and said, "No."

I felt sick to my stomach, so I ran to the bathroom. It reeked of urine and vomit, and I added to it. I started throwing up. Pria ran in and held my hair. Binita was there and was laughing. I staggered around and couldn't figure out why she was laughing. I told Pria I wanted to go home. She grabbed our purses, and we went outside. She got us a tuk tuk and we went home. I fell on my bed, in my clothes and slept.

When I wake up it is the afternoon. I walk out to the kitchen and fix a chia. My stomach still feels funny. Binita must have put something in the coke for sure. Sapna came out with just a robe barely tied around her. You could see her panties. Gyan was right behind her. She gave me a wink.

I was disgusted. If this is what *going out* and being a sophisticated woman is all about, I don't want to be one.

WHAT AM I DOING HERE?

After only two months living with these other girls, I am not sure I can stay much longer. They are obsessed with being modern women, Westernized. I don't want what they are offering. I like my quiet Indian life that I had in the Leper Colony, especially after my papa died and I didn't have to have sex with those old men anymore.

I am not like these other girls. I don't need movies, or famous people to follow. I don't need to wear the latest fashion clothes or make-up. I've invited them to a Bible study that Joy does on Sunday afternoons, and I've tried to tell these girls about Jesus, but they just laugh. Pria is nice and says once she is married, she will worship this Jesus along with Ganesh, her primary god. I tried to explain the difference, but she didn't want to hear.

I miss my mam and my little brother. I can't say that I miss Sumit because I haven't seen him in so many years.

Sometimes I wonder if he is still alive.

My mam did come to know Jesus. It was a sweet moment.

Before I left the Colony, Joshua had gathered some of us who follow Jesus to have a Bible study. I invited my mam to come with me. Joshua talked about the woman at the well. I had not heard this story before.

Joshua was saying, "This woman had many husbands, and she was living with a man who was not her husband."

I looked over at my mam, she was listening intently. By the end of the story, my mam was weeping.

She stood up and asked, "This Jesus knows us, knows what we have done and still loves us?"

"Yes," said Joshua, "Would you like to know this Jesus?"

My mam said yes, and Joshua led her in a prayer. I could see that the Holy Spirit had touched her heart. She looked up at me smiling. Then she started crying and hugging me.

She was saying "This peace is so overwhelming. Oh Latika, I am so sorry, so sorry. Can you ever forgive me?" She kept weeping and saying this over and over.

I took her hand and looked her straight in the eye. "Mam, I forgave you and Papa years ago. Jesus has forgiven you too. Mam, I love you."

It was the first time I ever remember my mam saying to me "Latika, I love you."

* * * * * * * * * * * * *

I am not doing well here in Mumbai. I pray every day,

"God give me strength, help me to do my work, help me to love my roommates."

I don't go out with them anymore.

I want to talk to Joy and Pooja, but I am afraid. I can't tell them about getting drunk. Or about these girls and the boys they bring home. What if Joy gets mad at me. Or what if he comes and thrashes these girls. My papa would have beat me for getting drunk or running around with boys if we had stayed in our village. Joy could throw me out and then where would I go?

Most of the time, I stay in my room, except when I am in the kitchen fixing my food. I was able to buy a computer at my company when they offered a discount. So, now I have downloaded Netflix and I do like watching movies in my room. I am safe there. I still don't understand everything I see in the movies. Some of them are violent and I don't usually watch those all the way to the end. I still don't like the culture I see in the movies. Men and women living together without being married. From what the other girls tell me, this is nothing like the American movies. I watched one once on Netflix. The Bollywood movies don't show nudity, and the couple if they are lying in bed together are fully clothed. They never kiss mouth-to-mouth, unless it is a short one at the end. Not so with the American movie. They were naked and rubbing against each other in the bed, kissing all over each other's bodies.

I fast-forwarded it wondering, "Why do we need to see that?"

My roommates have parties almost every weekend. They bring guys to our apartment. Everyone is drinking.

I ask Joy and Pooja if I can stay with them on Saturday and Sunday. I tell them it would be easier to go to church, Bible studies and help out with ministry, but the truth is that I don't want to be here. They are gracious and say I can stay with them.

I love going to church with them. We go on Saturday evenings and all-day Sunday. Some Saturday afternoons we go to a neighborhood, and we hand out tracks to people walking on the street. Sometimes we pass out food to those living on the streets. And sometimes Joy has blankets and clothes we can give to those who are homeless. It feels good to help others. We tell them about Jesus and that He is the light they need. It is joyous when some accept Him. We take them to the church and Joy helps them to find a job and training.

Joy has a school. It is a very nice school with about 200 students. On my days off, I will go to the school and sit with the children. It would be fun to be a teacher. I ask Joy if I could be a teacher. He tells me that it requires that I go to the university and get a degree. I probably don't have the money to do that, but Joy thinks there may be scholarships.

I am messing up at work. I am not meeting my quota. I am sure they will fire me.

Every time a boy stops at my cubicle, I want to scream at him to leave me alone. There is one, Derek, who keeps asking me to go out with him. He waits for me after work in the stairwell. He walks with me, and I try to walk away from him.

"Come on Latika, just go to dinner with me. All I want to do is to talk to you."

I just shake my head no. And I run out of the building. He hasn't followed me yet. I hope he doesn't.

I know that Jesus is with me, but I am so lonely. Life is so very different here. If I go back home to the Leper Colony, at least I will know what to expect. I can live with Mam in our one room. Since our place to stay doesn't cost anything, maybe I could save some money to move us out of the Colony someday. Or maybe Joshua would help me to get a teaching degree and I could teach the children in the Colony. I bet he would really like it if I came home.

I know Mam would. The last time I talked to her she sounded so sad and weak. She didn't say much. I know she misses Papa. I know Ashok tries to help her, but he is so young. She never talks about Sumit. I wonder if she misses him or tries to find out where he is. I know she feels all alone. I miss her.

Maybe if I go home, I can get a job in Jaipur at a call center or some other place. Ashok probably needs my help. Mam can't cook any more since her fingers are just nubs. Where is Ashok getting his food? Who is helping him with his schoolwork? Is he staying out of trouble? He has not been around the last few times I talk to Mam and she just says that he is fine. But is he? Or is Mam just trying to protect me?

Life would be easier if I just go back to Jaipur and live in the Leper Colony. At least, I would know what to expect and can live a simple life.

My phone is buzzing. It is Joshua again. I am too upset. I can't answer his call right now.

I don't want to be here in Mumbai anymore. That's it, I am going home.

Going Home

I have enough money saved for the one-way ticket back to Jaipur. But, again, only for a third-class ticket. At least I know this time what to expect and I am ready for the journey.

I have all my belongings packed in one big bag. I also made myself some food.

I didn't have the courage to tell Joy and Pooja. I left them a note at the church. I also left a note for my boss because I didn't have the nerve to tell him. What if he calls the Powells and tells them that I was too dumb to do the job? Mrs. Powell will be so very disappointed in me. I don't think I can take the shame. I don't think my roommates will notice; they will probably be glad I left.

I texted Joshua late last night. Will he be disappointed too? Will he be angry? I hope that he gets my text about meeting me at the train station. I hope he will be there. I don't have anyone else to call.

The ride back is uneventful. Not much different than

the first time I rode the train. This time I know what to expect and I brought enough food with me so that I don't have to leave the station at the stops or buy from a vendor. It's very early, 5:00 am, when the train arrives at the station at Jaipur.

This station is old and run down. It is not like the shiny new one in Mumbai. It stinks. It reeks of urine. Homeless people are sitting on the benches sleeping, many of them do not have shoes on. Their hair is all matted and they are dirty. I've never noticed them before. Is that because that used to be me? Or maybe God is changing my heart to see those in desperate need.

I walk outside the train station. I don't see Joshua.

I wonder, "Maybe he was too mad when he got my text, and he won't come. What should I do?" Then I think to myself, "I will just sit down and wait for him to show up."

I feel so relieved to be out of the city and heading back to the Colony, even though it is dirty compared to where I have been. I can't wait to hug my mam. I didn't call her to tell her I was leaving. I didn't want her to be disappointed that I left a good job. I also want to see Ashok. I have missed him. But I also want to surprise both of them.

I begin to wonder if Joshua received my text. Or maybe he is really very angry with me. I did not hear back from him before my phone battery died. Should I try to walk home? I am not sure how to get to the Colony. I look around for someone who may be able to help and give me direction, but I don't want them to know that I am looking for the Leper Colony. I could get a tuk tuk but I wouldn't know how to tell them where to go. I could say to take me to the big mall, but he would know that I don't belong there and refuse to take me.

As I'm looking around, my heart leaps for joy when I see Joshua and Asha coming toward me. I run to them. They grab me and give me a big hug. They don't seem mad, which is a relief.

"Thank you for coming and picking me up," I practically blurt out. "I didn't know if you got my text because my phone died."

Joshua nodded, "Yes we got it and replied that we would be here to get you. Sorry we were late. You know how congested the traffic can be."

I ask with hope in my heart, "Will you take me to the Colony now so I can see Mam and Ashok?"

Joshua steps aside and Asha grasps my hand and says, "You must be really tired from your trip, so we're going to our house so you can rest."

It seems unusual that they are not taking me to Mam right away. Maybe she is too sick to see me. I don't ask any more questions because I am grateful that they came and picked me up, and that they do not seem angry or disappointed with me.

I don't talk much on the way to Joshua's house. I feel the breeze from the partially open car window, and I drift in and out of sleep on the long ride home.

The next thing I feel is Asha stroking my hair and gently saying, "We are home. We have a place for you to come in and rest."

She takes me to a room in their house that has two twin beds. I lay down on one of the beds and I sleep deeply for several hours. When I wake up, I go to find Joshua and Asha. I walk out into the living room that has two small brown couches. One couch that is also a bed has a lamp for lighting next to it. Joshua and Asha are sitting on one of the couches talking. She sees me and immediately asks if I want something to drink or eat. I decline since it is not dinner time. She encourages me to sit on the couch across from them.

I sit down and Joshua looks at me softly. Taking my hands in his, he says, "Latika, your mam got really sick while you were gone. She went to Heaven two days ago. We tried to call you but there was no answer."

I sit back in my seat in shock. I don't know what to say. I don't know how to react. I feel deeply overcome with sadness. I didn't get to tell her good-bye. I will not get to hug her. I know I should be happy that she went to Heaven.

I put my face in my hands and start to cry, which feels strange because I don't usually let myself feel anything. It's too painful to really deal with how I feel. The tears just feel good as they stream hotly down my face. Asha comes over and sits by me. She puts her arm around me. After several minutes I look up at her.

Through my tears, I ask Joshua, "Will I see her again when I go to Heaven?"

A big and kind smile broadens over his face, "Yes, you will be with her in Heaven someday."

NEW BEGINNINGS

Joshua and Asha are so kind to me. I feel something in my heart that I have not experienced before. I feel peace. My heart aches because my mam is not here, but I feel relief talking to Joshua.

Joshua tells me that Ashok is now at a boarding school in Tonk. This used to be an orphanage and that is what it really is. But the government doesn't allow orphanages in India anymore, so now they are called boarding schools. He is with other boys and Joshua says he gets the highest marks in his class. He will stay there until he graduates in five years. I will get to go see him this weekend.

Later that evening, I go with Asha to the market to get food for dinner. Joshua is talking to a couple who showed up at their door asking for help. When we return, the couple is gone. Joshua had given them some food packets, clothes and told them about Jesus.

I help Asha cook dinner in her tiny kitchen. I take all the food out and sit it on the dining table that sits behind the couches in the big room. Joshua is sitting at the table.

Asha comes out with the water glasses and we both sit down with him.

Joshua says a blessing. He thanks God for my safe journey back. He asks God to comfort me. Then he thanks God for the meal. It is a beautiful prayer spoken with love and joy.

I am moved to tears that fall softly down my cheeks.

I look at Joshua and say, "I know I have disappointed you and the Powells. I know I should have stayed but I just couldn't stay there any longer. It was too hard."

Joshua looks me square in the eye and says, "I am not disappointed and the Powells will not be either. Most importantly, God is not disappointed with you."

"Latika, you are not a failure, you have done nothing wrong. In fact, I know that God has a plan for you."

I bow my head and look down at my plate. I'm not sure how to receive this.

Even though I know Jesus has saved me, I still felt dirty and bad most days. I feel like I need to work hard to gain approval. Before she was saved, Mam constantly reminded me that Papa had leprosy because of his past lives, and something he did to deserve leprosy, and that we must have contributed to it since we were with him. Leprosy meant being kicked out of Naniji's house, walking to village after village to find a place to stay, and spending time with men who I did not want to be with doing things that felt wrong to me. I thought I made this bad thing happen. I thought I had done something wrong in a past life that caused me to feel this uncomfortable inside, like there was something wrong with me.

Tears begin streaming down my face. I don't really

understand why. Something is shifting inside me. I know in my heart that it is okay to show Joshua and Asha that I'm crying.

I look up at him and say, "Something is happening inside of me that I don't understand. You and Asha make me feel so at home and protected. This is very different from anything I have felt in the past. Are you saying that I don't have to do good works to gain God's favor? I mean, I know that I am saved, I know Jesus and believe in Him, but I still feel that I need to do something, lots of things, to make God happy."

Joshua and Asha nod and look at me with a love I never saw from my mam, papa or brothers.

Joshua explains, "Latika, there is nothing you have to do to gain God's love. He loves you no matter what. He made you and He will be your father and take care of you."

Asha says, "We want you to live with us. We want to take care of you. Our sons have left the house for college. There is space for you."

I remember the time that I expected our new home in a Leper Colony to have rooms and furniture. Instead, our home had a hard concrete floor and no privacy. Now, Joshua and his wife want me to live with them in my own room with a real door that closes!

I'm still processing this information. I wonder out loud, "But what will I do? Can I get a job?"

Then, Joshua says, "What you have been through will help others. You can teach children. Your love for learning can inspire others to learn." Joshua continued, "Don't forget Jesus' love. So many people don't know about it. You can share and teach them that."

I think of how Jesus died on the cross for me. Someone drove stakes through His hands and feet. When He was hanging on the cross He couldn't breathe. It was a painfully slow death, and He did this because He loved me. And, He loves others. And yes, I do want people to know how much He loves them.

I look at Joshua and Asha and say, "Thank you. Thank you for giving me a real, loving home. I have longed for it for many years."

THREE YEARS LATER

I have lived with Joshua and Asha for three years. They have helped me complete my requirements at the Jaipur National University where I have received a teaching degree. I am stunned at how different my life is and how much joy I feel in the depths of my heart. I understand the love of Jesus in a totally different way than I ever have before.

Joshua has hired me to be the teacher in the Leper Colony. I love these children and I can understand what they have suffered. Many of them, because they were born in the colony, have never been to a school. We are starting with the basics. And each day I get to tell them about Jesus and His love for them. I get to hug, encourage them and watch as their bright eyes open up to learn new things. I think they like someone showing that they care. I am teaching some of the older girls to sew so they can take in jobs and not have to beg on the streets or be a prostitute. Also, I get to help these girls who, like me, were forced into prostitution by their fathers. I share my experience with them and I encourage them to come to school. Joshua is trying to help the fathers see that this is not a life for their daughters. It is a very slow process.

Recently, Joshua introduced me to Zach, a missionary who moved to India from Dubai to help teach the children. Zach has rich black hair and caring brown eyes. The first time I met Zach I felt attracted to him, but I also felt uncomfortable. I wondered if he was like those men who Papa brought around to me. I avoided talking to him, but he kept being really nice to me.

Joshua and Asha would invite him to their house many nights for dinner. So, we have been able to talk and learn about his family and life in Dubai. I don't talk much on those nights. I just listen.

Joshua told me last week that Zach said he wanted to arrange a marriage with me. Joshua asked me if I would please pray about it. I asked Joshua if Zach knew about my past, thinking that if he did, he wouldn't want me. But Joshua explained to me that he told Zach what my papa did to me, and he assured me that Zach understood and wanted to marry me anyway.

I remember Asha's story about how her Bible director wanted to arrange for her marriage to Joshua, but her father wanted to arrange her marriage to a wealthy man. She took a week to fast and pray. Then, she knew she was to marry Joshua. So, I asked Joshua if I could fast and pray for a week. A knowing smile crossed his face and he readily agreed.

After that week, I felt it was the right thing to do and told Joshua. He spoke to Zach and one evening brought Zach to the house. He asked Zach and me to sit on the couch and to talk to each other. Zach looked at me with his smiling eyes. He looked kind, not like the men who my father had set me up with.

He asked, "Latika, what do you think about getting married to me?"

I blinked, "Well, I have fasted and prayed. I think it is the right thing to do."

"But," he asked, "Are you attracted to me? Because I am very attracted to you. You are kind, and you love the Lord. I watch you with the children and I know that you will be a good mother someday. I would be honored to have you as my wife."

Stunned, I stammer, "Thank you. I am not used to men being so kind to me. Yes, I think you are very handsome. You are so gentle and kind to the children. I love watching you play with them."

"I know Joshua has told you about my past. Are you sure this is what you want?"

Zach replied, "Latika, I know what your papa did. It was horrible and I am so sorry that this happened to you. I promise to protect you. And if God allows us to have a daughter, I promise to protect her and her sister too! I will not allow any men to harm them."

We went on to talk for an hour and then Joshua came into the room. He and his wife sat down on the couch. "So, Latika and Zach, can I arrange this marriage?"

We look at each other and then turn to Joshua and say in unison, "Yes."

"Great," exclaims Joshua, "We will have the wedding in two days!"

Outcast No More

I am sitting in the side room at the church building in Tonk. It is also the school where Ashok lives. This is where Zach and I will be married. I am wearing a long white wedding gown. I feel blessed but mostly I feel redeemed.

I will walk down the aisle of the church with Joshua by my side. Ashok will be standing by Zach. In a few minutes, I will be married. I'm not sure what to expect, but Joshua says Zach will take care of me. And I trust both of them. Sometimes, I still wonder a little about the future. So many times I thought I would find a new place of security, but my hopes were dashed.

Alone right now before it all starts, I bow my head and raise my palms up to offer a prayer to Jesus.

"Jesus, thank You. I pray this will be different. I have strived to find joy in everything in my life in spite of fear, disappointment and depression. Thank you, Jesus, for carrying me through. I have lived through many disappointments, but I count them all for joy because You have been faithful to take care of me. I trust You to take care of me as I start a new life with Zach."

"I know we will face hard times and persecution because we live in India. This area has been a wasteland, not just because it is in the desert, but because so many who have tried to spread Your light have been killed here. It is a graveyard of missionaries. Persecution is ahead of us. Strengthen Zach and me so that we will stand. Give us Your power to remain strong and be light in this very dark place."

"And Father, I thank You that I am no longer an outcast. Instead, I have a place and a people that I belong to. I thank You that I am a child of Yours, a friend of Joshua and Asha, and a wife to Zach. I thank You for giving me a place to belong."

My brethren, count it all joy when you fall into various trials

James 1:2, NKJV

An Afterword

I am writing this story to tell the horribly unfair saga of how lepers are treated in India. They live a victimized, oppressed, and persecuted life. Most people think that leprosy is a disease of the past, that was eradicated years ago. I can tell you that leprosy is real and is still prevalent today.

According to the World Health Organization, over 200,000 new cases of leprosy are reported from 160 countries worldwide every year. India accounts for 60 percent of these global cases. It is estimated that in India, over one million people live with visible deformities due to leprosy. Also, these people live marginalized lives in over 700 leper colonies. I have visited four of these colonies in different cities in India. In 2014, we started working with one in Jaipur.

Leprosy attacks the nervous system. The leper's hands become numb and small muscles become paralyzed. They lose the ability to feel. Repeated nerve damage and infection can cause paralysis of small muscles leading the finger or toe bones to "claw" and to shorten. Serious, untreated wounds lead to amputations.

If the facial nerve is affected, a person loses the eye's blinking reflex, preventing proper closure of the lid and protection of the eye. This eventually leads to blindness.

The symptoms may occur within one year but can take as long as twenty years or even more to appear. In India, the mortality rate for leprosy is approximately four times greater than the general population.

It's a horrific disease. And so, people with leprosy continue to suffer. Greatly. And yes, leprosy is entirely curable with multidrug therapy, a combination of three antibiotics.

The World Health Organization provides free medicine to India for treating and curing leprosy. That leprosy can be prevented, treated, and cured makes it challenging to understand why leprosy is so prevalent in India. But understanding that India is 80 percent Hindu, and thinks of itself as a Hindu nation, is critical to understanding why the disease is rampant in this country.

When someone in India contracts leprosy, their religion labels them as a person with *bad karma*.

Karma is the belief that what you did in a past life is the reason for your circumstances in this life. So if you get leprosy, it is because you did something very bad in a previous life. As a Hindu, it becomes your duty to suffer well and hope to be reincarnated to a better place in the next life. No one will help you because it will change karma. When a person's karma is changed, it is a risk that in the next life, that person will have to repeat the suffering. If someone helps someone change their position to a better life, they too may suffer bad karma in their next life. It's a sticky wicket.

India's culture is honor and shame-based, as are most countries in the Middle East and Asia. In these cultures, a person must do everything he/she can, to maintain their own honor and the family honor to avoid public shame. Lying, hiding, stealing are common. The caste system is engrained in India's culture and belief system and only furthers this culture of shame.

These beliefs impact people who contract leprosy. They are forced out of their homes, even by their loved ones because they have brought shame on the entire family. They leave with nothing but the clothes they are wearing. They are shunned from the community and forced to beg for food every day.

As their children grow up, they are rejected and not allowed to go to school. These children learn how to beg or steal. Some of the children are prostituted by their parents. Often, the children never get the disease. However, most of the children never leave the colony because they do not know another way of life.

Because this culture and its practices are difficult for westerners to understand, I hope to give you some insight into the lives of those who find themselves trapped in a Leper Colony in India.

This is a work of fiction based on true stories I have encountered on my many journeys to India. I am not using my real name, or the real names of the people I know, because at the writing of this book, the government of India is ruled by the BJP party. This party is comprised of militant Hindus. When the Prime Minister took office several years ago, he stated that he wanted India to be 100 percent Hindu by 2020. 2020 has come and gone and the country is still only 79.8 percent Hindu. But this has not stopped persecution.

I am also not using my real name to protect myself and those we work with in India. Several years ago, *Compassion International* and *World Vision* were kicked out of India. Many people who work for these two organizations lost their jobs, as did the children and people who they helped. As of this writing, *Greenpeace* and *Amnesty International* can no longer provide funding in India. We know Christians who have been missionaries for years who have not been allowed to stay. Some who came back to the West on furlough, and had years left on their visas, were denied reentry at Customs.

So I write this book under a pen name. Because if I am found out, I would not be allowed back into the country.

–The Author

For more information about how to help provide food to those with leprosy in India and education for the children in the leper colony go to *http://nexusforgood.org*.